BETTER *Man*

Rebecca Skovgaard

Whimsical Publications, LLC

Florida

Better Man is a work of fiction. Names, characters, and incidents are the products of the author's imagination and are either fictitious or are used fictitiously. Any resemblance to actual events or persons, living or dead, is entirely coincidental.

If you purchased this book without a cover, you should be aware that this book may have been stolen property and reported as "unsold and destroyed" to the publisher. In such case, neither the publisher nor the author has received payment for this "stripped book."

To purchase the authorized electronic edition of *Better Man*, visit
www.whimsicalpublications.com

Cover art by Traci Markou
Editing by Brieanna Robertson
Proofed by Eden Royce

Published in the United States by
Whimsical Publications, LLC
Florida

ISBN-13: 978-1-940707-92-1

Fuck. No, that wasn't right. *Good.* Her having a boyfriend was good.

Canaan stayed quiet, watching her. He planted his feet and crossed his arms over his chest, and she kept looking, as though maybe she liked the way that position stretched the short sleeves of his tee over the bulge of his biceps or something. The effect was entirely unintentional, not like when she'd done the same and put her damn breasts on display for him.

Anyway, she shouldn't be looking. She had a *boyfriend*.

She acted like that was supposed to mean something to him. "Yeah?"

"He wants to have sex."

Quelle surprise. Unless he was a *fucking eunuch*.

Wait. Maybe he'd get to kill the dude.

She walked closer, just a little into the light. She stood at the side of his favorite recliner and rubbed her fingers over the leather on its back.

He could imagine those fingers moving over his skin in the same way.

Then she shamed him by looking up into his eyes and letting him see—fear, hurt. Woundedness.

"I haven't…"

Shit. He was pretty sure he didn't want to hear this.

"I haven't had sex with anyone since…"

He finished for her, compelled against his will to put her out of her misery. "Since you were raped as a child?"

"It wasn't rape."

"Yes, it was, Josefina. Unless he was fifteen, too. And likely even then."

She wrapped her arms around herself again, but it was defensive this time. She wasn't yanking his chain with it. Looking at her feet, she shook her head. "Thirteen. And he wasn't."

Jesus. "Was it incest?"

She shook her head again. "Not exactly. He was my mother's boyfriend."

Unsurprised, he nodded. Feeling the tug of it, he was pretty sure she'd never told another soul. Except perhaps her worthless piece of shit mother, who clearly hadn't put herself out to protect her daughter. Obviously, it had gone on for years.

"Do you still have to see him? Face him?"

"He comes 'round my mother sometimes. If she's got drugs or booze and he doesn't. I don't go there anymore. I don't…see my mother."

Sef looked a lot like she needed a hug, but it was entirely possible that the last thing she wanted would be a man's touch. And he'd be the last guy to offer one. Still, his fingers flexed. They wanted to hold her. Or kill the bastard who'd hurt her—one or the other. Both, really.

He took a deep, steadying breath. "Is your boyfriend pressing you?" 'Cause maybe that one could still use killing, too.

She was quiet for a minute. "Trevor. No, but..." She chewed her lip, then looked up at him. Didn't lift her head, but merely peeked up from under her lashes. "I wanted to ask if you would..."

Suddenly, he was dead certain he didn't want to hear what was coming.

"If you would...make love to me."

"Christ. You're an idiot." He tore his fingers through his hair, then walked away from her. He left her there in that circle of light and went to stare out into the dark. Except his gaze didn't go there. It focused on the pane instead. Where he could see her reflection—her back still turned to him, her head still bowed.

After a long silence, she turned and raised her head. "It would mean a lot to me. I'd really like to know... I'd like to try it with someone I can trust."

He looked into the reflection of her eyes. "If you can't trust Trevor then you shouldn't be thinking of doing what you're thinking of doing with him."

She walked over and stood behind him, enough to the side that their gazes could connect in the glass. "I have to, some-time. I *want* to. I want to know if...if I can be normal that way."

Canaan dropped his head and pressed, forehead and palms, against the window.

"I want it to be you, Canaan."

He shook his head. It was possible his whole body shook.

"I'm not the right man for that. It's crazy anyway, but even if it wasn't, I'm not the right one."

"I think you are. You'd be gentle."

He let out a breath in a scoff.

She touched his shoulder. "You'd stop if I needed you to."

Not fucking likely. Canaan pulled away and crossed the room, as far away as he could get, into the dark. He was silently pleading with his dick to stay put. "It's not gonna happen. Sef, you're crazy to think it."

$\mathscr{A}$CKNOWLEDGEMENTS

To *Chi Daug*.

To the strong women and men, those I know and those I don't, who survive what humans shouldn't have to endure and still find peace and love in their hearts.

Also by
REBECCA SKOVGAARD

Tynie's Place

Happy Man
Lucky Man

CHAPTER ONE

"I know where you were last night."

Canaan Liberty stifled a groan, mostly, as he rolled over. He could see a bit of light peeking around the edges of the drapes. Bright, Nashville in June light. Maybe it wasn't as early in the morning as it felt.

"Yeah? Then you should know I'd still be sleeping off those last couple shots I had."

"It's damn near noon. Joss said you were coming back today. I probably saved you missing your flight."

Canaan grunted into the phone. Will Hunter was a fine friend, but still—a couple too many shots. He remembered now why he'd quit drinking. *Really* drinking, he meant. Well, there'd been a lot about that.

"Anyway, congratulations, dude. And why didn't I know this about you?"

"I don't know, man—you're the detective. Besides, do I know everything about you?"

"You know my dog, my wife, my baby, my job, my phobia, and that I can't dribble left-handed for shit. So, *yeah*, pretty much."

"Yeah, well—"

"Faith Hill kissed you. On the mouth. And Tim was standing right there."

"Music video of the year, man. She was pretty happy. Grateful."

"I can't believe you wrote that song. Or that you're in Nashville accepting an award for it, and I find out about it when I see you smooching Faith."

"She was smooching me." Canaan rolled out of bed, rubbing his face. Will *was* a good friend, and he had a point. Friends told friends about these kinds of things. Just because Canaan hadn't had a friend—or been worthy of one—for the last few years didn't mean he shouldn't recognize one when it happened. Or act like he knew it. He pulled the drapes open and blinked into the light. "You're right. I'm sorry, man. It's only...you know, I like things simple. I come down here, I see these guys with talent and money, and their lives aren't simple. They have friends who aren't friends, lovers they don't even like, and wives who cheat on them. They're surrounded by losers and users."

Looking out the window, he watched the Cumberland River glint in the sun. He knew that, a few blocks behind him, the cleaning crew was mucking out the Bridgestone Arena, and thousands of folks who worked in country music were nursing their sore heads and already looking for the next big hit. He'd learned most guests at the hotel wanted the city view. He wanted the river. And, better yet, he wanted to be home, on the farm he worked for Joss and Marta, a couple of lovely women who wanted nothing from him but some help in the barn and a little quiet...friendship.

"I don't want to live like that. So I don't talk about it much. It's no big secret—Joss and Marta know. It just never came up between you and me."

A pause on the line let him know Will was considering his words. That was Will's way. He could accept another man's point of view, but he'd give it some thought first. "I get it. Leet's the same way—a star quarterback can get a lot of attention, and it ain't all pretty. But it's cool knowing. You've written some of my favorite songs."

"What, you finally got around to googling me, Deputy?"

"I did, in fact. Since I learned your last name from the TV."

"You only had to ask."

"Yeah, well, sometimes when a guy doesn't share a thing like that, we're both better off with me not knowing."

Canaan supposed that was true.

"Anyway," Will added. "When you get back, I've got a CD for you to sign. Now that you've kissed Faith on national television, you'll probably go somewhere."

Canaan laughed as he closed the phone. Where he wanted to go was home, and, *yeah*, he was damn close to missing his flight.

For a lot of years, Josefina Claire had known exactly what she wanted. At thirteen, she wanted to be safe in her home and not have to worry about being caught alone in the house with her mother's volatile, drunken boyfriend. At sixteen, she wanted to give a decent life to the baby she hadn't asked for and couldn't support. At twenty, she wanted to sleep somewhere besides her aunt's couch, and a better way out of grueling poverty and soul-killing jobs than she could get by attending community college part-time.

At twenty-two, she wanted to go to medical school.

And at nearly twenty-three, she wanted Canaan Liberty. Well, technically speaking, she'd wanted him since she was twenty-one, when she'd first met him.

She was getting better at getting what she wanted.

In fact, since she was sixteen, she hadn't failed at it. Except for the Canaan thing, and she was devoting her attention to that right now.

Seffie would be the first to say she'd been blessed with a lot of help. Foremost, there was Sadie Benjamin, a young midwife with welcoming arms Seffie had met when she was fifteen and pregnant. Sadie didn't make her feel shamed for the situation she was in, one that Seffie couldn't help. She didn't try to force Seffie to reveal who had fathered her baby. She'd given support and respect and, best of all, a loving home for baby Constantino.

Then there was Leet Hayes, who married Sadie and took Tino and Sadie's adopted son Jace into his heart and home. Seffie knew it was Leet behind Sadie's gentle request for a formal adoption when Tino was five. Leet was a man and, more than anything, Seffie knew he was trying to protect his woman from a broken heart.

Seffie gave her consent. She knew it would have broken Tino's heart, too, if she'd tried to take him back. She'd made the right choice, having gotten the most important of the things that she wanted—a safe, loving place for her son. She was a part of that family now, too, and it was far, far more than she could have expected.

Leet's parents were top cardiologists at a major medical center. Doctor Aletha Hayes had taken Seffie under her wing—becoming a better mother to her, Leet claimed, than

she'd been to her own two sons. That got Seffie most everything else she wanted. She had a safe home with her own
bedroom—that once was Leet's—a year at an Ivy League college, and admission into a highly regarded medical school.

She was down to that single item on her list.

She'd met Canaan at Sadie's wedding. Canaan had
danced with her, but that wasn't saying much. There'd been
dancing at the party on the night before the wedding and at
the reception after, and he'd been in the midst of a gaggle of
women throughout both occasions. The man had moves, and
he had absolutely no difficulty keeping a handful of women
happy on the dance floor.

When the women had ended that first evening down at
the Easy Rider, they'd all agreed that Canaan was every bit
as hot as the exotic dancers, Bill Blade and Lance Duguid,
without even taking his clothes off. There was also some
conjecture that he was making a determined effort to keep
his attention away from Seffie's hot little self. That was Joss's
term, not hers. And when Joss—one of Sadie's mothers—was
handing out condoms to those she figured would need them
the most, well, the majority went to Sadie's friend, Kate.
Deputy Will had watched over the whole group, but it was
obvious who really held his interest, so they'd all seen that
coming. But Joss kept one back for Seffie, just in case Canaan did more than pretend not to look.

He didn't. Not that night, or at the wedding the next day,
or at Will and Kate's wedding a few months later. Or the
handful of times she'd seen him since at the Hayes or Hunter
family get-togethers for birthdays and christenings.

The man was wickedly appealing. He was a compact,
tightly muscled five-eleven. He moved with grace and preda-
tory stealth. His hair was dark enough almost to be black and
nearly reached his shoulders. He usually wore it held back
with a bandana. His eyes were the same shade and intensely
observant. He seldom spoke, but it was clear he processed
everything, missed nothing.

Except that, around her, he seemed to be Captain Oblivious. He treated her like a little sister—a twelve-year-old little
sister. One who was an obligatory nuisance. He always
greeted her, meeting her gaze for a brief moment, giving her
a nod. But then he'd be on to someone else—tossing Tino up

over his shoulder, talking football with Jace or Leet, wrestling with Will's dog Beowulf...really, anyone or anything seemed to hold more appeal than she did.

Seffie had declared it enough. It wasn't like the man had another woman. He didn't. He lived in a small A-frame on Joss and Marta's farm. He helped out on the farm, taking care of the animals and doing the heavier work. He practiced tai chi on his front porch and worked out with his *bō* staff in the barn. He disappeared for a handful of days every two or three months—and there was a mystery Seffie would have to solve. Other than that, he was alone in his house every damn night.

She was going to find a way to change that.

"Canaan."

Dammit. She with the hot little body had nearly startled him. And he *never* startled.

Leave it to her.

Canaan barely kept from bobbling his bags. He'd parked his truck down at the barn, so he hadn't had the benefit of his headlights sweeping across his front porch. And he'd stopped on his way home to have a couple beers with Will and Kate—celebrating his CMT award with his friends, like a normal person would do. But he couldn't claim he was impaired—if he was, Deputy Will would surely have him sleeping it off in the spare bedroom of his old Victorian down the in village.

And, yeah, it was dark, moonless, and she'd tucked herself into one of the wooden rockers at the far end of the porch.

Still. He'd only missed her because it was, *well*—her.

Josefina.

A boyhood of emulating his grandfather's Choctaw traditions and honing nature skills. More than a decade of tai chi practice and martial arts discipline. Years of Ranger training. *Eons* of living on the edge, of sleeping with an eye open, of relying on constant, full awareness of his surroundings in order to survive.

She was barely more than a girl, and she blew it all to

hell. She was his own personal flashbang. He was blinded around her, all his senses stunned into uselessness.

Good thing he wasn't living any place more dangerous than a damn goat farm. He'd have never survived his years on the ground in Afghanistan if she'd been around.

It had been like that from the start. He'd met her at Leet and Sadie's wedding party. She'd been wearing this little red dress that he couldn't even *look* at. She shimmered—all of her. That damn dress, her tight, curvaceous body. Her long dark hair that curled bright and a little red in ringlets, those surprising blue eyes.

Canaan liked to dance, and the group was friendly and happy enough that there was never a shortage of women out on the dance floor. He danced with Josefina, yes, he did. But never alone, never exactly even face to face with her, to say nothing of body to body.

He was pretty sure if that had happened, he'd have ended up tossing her over his shoulder and hauling her off to the nearest bed. Or cave. Grunting, and taking down anyone who got in his way. Dragging his knuckles on the ground and not caring who saw it.

But she was a damn kid.

It was clear she'd seen some hurt. You could see it in those big blues if you looked. She'd had a baby when she was still a baby herself, and he'd been around enough to know that when no one knew who your kid's dad was, it was someone it shouldn't be. She'd done the stand-up thing and given the baby up into loving and capable arms. That surely was the stand-up thing, but it fucking took some grit.

The girl had cojones.

Still, she was wounded. Despite her smiles, her intelligence, and her basically bright nature.

He could see it.

Shadows of grief and hurt lurking deep down in those eyes. Knowledge. That unwanted, unasked for, gut-rending understanding of true pain.

He could and should recognize it. He saw it in the mirror every day.

She was wounded. He was wounded. And two wounds didn't make a right.

He'd gotten better. It looked like she'd gotten better, too.

But still.

He took a couple breaths and tried to find stillness, his center, before he looked at her. "Josefina. What are you doing here?"

He kept his place dark. He felt safer relying on his night vision rather than the false security—and interference—of artificial light. But he could see her now. She uncurled herself from the chair, and somebody as little as she shouldn't have to spend so long doing it, or look so lithe and graceful in the midst of it.

She stepped close. Too close.

"Where have you been?"

"I was down at Will and Kate's, having a beer."

Even in the dark he could see those damn eyes. She knew his words were deliberate misinformation. She lifted an eyebrow—a dark, nicely-shaped one. "For three days?"

He didn't have to tell her every damn thing. Even things a normal guy would tell his friends. Josefina wasn't a friend and wasn't going to be. "My family all lives out of state."

The blasted woman recognized that, as well, for the misdirection it was. That brow stayed hooked up there like she was sniffing something a little off. Like it was an offense for him to keep anything from her.

"Why are you here, Sef?"

"I need to ask you something."

He sighed, and against every instinct he had—too little, too late—he opened the door. He motioned her in and very deliberately did not watch her move ahead of him, did not watch her ass as it—*dammit all.*

She took a few steps into his dark house. She knew her way around. He had kitchen and dining area to the left, with the living room and his bedroom beyond to the right. Above, there was an open loft. Her son Tino had slept up there, back in the day when Sadie had first brought him and Jace to live in Vermont.

Sef had spent some time in this house, visiting her son. Canaan had moved in when Sadie married Leet and the whole gang went to live at Leet's place. He hadn't changed much. It wasn't like he'd had a bunch of his own furniture out in that room off the barn he'd been squatting in.

Sadie's old stuff was fine with him. It wasn't something

he cared about.

But it probably wasn't right to expect Josefina to be comfortable in the dark, so he walked around her and turned on a low table lamp.

She looked up at him and swallowed. Whatever it was, she was nervous about it.

"We're friends, aren't we?"

"No."

Josefina wanted to stomp her foot. Could he be any more difficult? "Come on. You're good friends with Leet and Will, aren't you? And I'm friends with them."

Canaan lifted a damn shoulder like he was bored. "Then go ask them whatever it is you want."

"I can't." There was a basic truth behind that, for one. And two, *so* not the point. She crossed her arms under her breasts and dared him to look.

She was petite, a quarter-inch or so short of five-three. But she had curves, and most guys would be interested in what that motion did to her breasts.

Not Captain Oblivious. Though he was no longer meeting her gaze either.

He did something with his shoulders again—it looked a lot like he was trying to slough off an annoying burden. He left her there in that small circle of light and went to the kitchen.

"Do you want some water?"

That was big of him. "Do you have any wine or beer?"

"No."

Lord, the man could be an ass.

He had a filtered water tap at the sink and filled a glass with it. He walked over to her, holding it out a little, like he might be offering it to her. When she didn't move for a long minute, he lifted it and took a swallow.

"I will have some. Thanks." She took the glass from his hand and drank from it. She held it to her lips perhaps a moment longer than she needed to, watching him over the rim, but she wasn't overly provocative about it. She didn't, like, turn it to sip from the same place his lips had been or anything.

Still, it caused a satisfyingly hot flare in his eyes. And he gave a dismissive shake of his head when she offered it back.

She suppressed a smile and set the glass on the table. Then she stepped around him and walked to the wall of windows that formed the front of the house. She looked out into the dark for a long moment before she turned to face him.

"I have a boyfriend."

Fuck. No, that wasn't right. *Good.* Her having a boyfriend was good.

Canaan stayed quiet, watching her. He planted his feet and crossed his arms over his chest, and she kept looking, as though maybe she liked the way that position stretched the short sleeves of his tee over the bulge of his biceps or something. The effect was entirely unintentional, not like when she'd done the same and put her damn breasts on display for him.

Anyway, she shouldn't be looking. She had a *boyfriend*.

She acted like that was supposed to mean something to him. "Yeah?"

"He wants to have sex."

Quelle surprise. Unless he was a *fucking eunuch*.

Wait. Maybe he'd get to kill the dude.

She walked closer, just a little into the light. She stood at the side of his favorite recliner and rubbed her fingers over the leather on its back.

He could imagine those fingers moving over his skin in the same way.

Then she shamed him by looking up into his eyes and letting him see—fear, hurt. Woundedness.

"I haven't..."

Shit. He was pretty sure he didn't want to hear this.

"I haven't had sex with anyone since..."

He finished for her, compelled against his will to put her out of her misery. "Since you were raped as a child?"

"It wasn't rape."

"Yes, it was, Josefina. Unless he was fifteen, too. And likely even then."

She wrapped her arms around herself again, but it was defensive this time. She wasn't yanking his chain with it. Looking at her feet, she shook her head. "Thirteen. And he wasn't."

Jesus. "Was it incest?"

She shook her head again. "Not exactly. He was my mother's boyfriend."

Unsurprised, he nodded. Feeling the tug of it, he was pretty sure she'd never told another soul. Except perhaps her worthless piece of shit mother, who clearly hadn't put herself out to protect her daughter. Obviously, it had gone on for years.

"Do you still have to see him? Face him?"

"He comes 'round my mother sometimes. If she's got drugs or booze and he doesn't. I don't go there anymore. I don't...see my mother."

Sef looked a lot like she needed a hug, but it was entirely possible that the last thing she wanted would be a man's touch. And he'd be the last guy to offer one. Still, his fingers flexed. They wanted to hold her. Or kill the bastard who'd hurt her—one or the other. Both, really.

He took a deep, steadying breath. "Is your boyfriend pressing you?" 'Cause maybe that one could still use killing, too.

She was quiet for a minute. "Trevor. No, but..." She chewed her lip, then looked up at him. Didn't lift her head, but merely peeked up from under her lashes. "I wanted to ask if you would..."

Suddenly, he was dead certain he didn't want to hear what was coming.

"If you would...make love to me."

"Christ. You're an idiot." He tore his fingers through his hair, then walked away from her. He left her there in that circle of light and went to stare out into the dark. Except his gaze didn't go there. It focused on the pane instead. Where he could see her reflection—her back still turned to him, her head still bowed.

After a long silence, she turned and raised her head. "It would mean a lot to me. I'd really like to know... I'd like to try it with someone I can trust."

He looked into the reflection of her eyes. "If you can't

trust Trevor then you shouldn't be thinking of doing what you're thinking of doing with him."

She walked over and stood behind him, enough to the side that their gazes could connect in the glass. "I have to, sometime. I *want* to. I want to know if...if I can be normal that way."

Canaan dropped his head and pressed, forehead and palms, against the window.

"I want it to be you, Canaan."

He shook his head. It was possible his whole body shook.

"I'm not the right man for that. It's crazy anyway, but even if it wasn't, I'm not the right one."

"I think you are. You'd be gentle."

He let out a breath in a scoff.

She touched his shoulder. "You'd stop if I needed you to."

Not fucking likely. Canaan pulled away and crossed the room, as far away as he could get, into the dark. He was silently pleading with his dick to stay put. "It's not gonna happen. Sef, you're crazy to think it."

Okay, the boyfriend part was a sham. But none of the rest of it was.

It was true, all too true, that Josefina wasn't sure if she'd ever find pleasure in lovemaking. She'd read about it, studied it clinically, talked with friends, saw it on TV and in movies—saw it in her friends Sadie and Kate with their handsome husbands. She knew it could be good—pleasurable and fun and...loving.And she was sure—really, truly sure—that if it would ever be good for her, it would be with Canaan.

He had some pain in him. He'd traveled some dark road, just like she had. She could see it when she looked into his eyes. Whatever happened when he touched her, however she reacted, he'd understand. And she'd be safe.

Deep, deep in her heart, Josefina was certain that the two of them were meant for each other. She figured she was a long way from convincing him of it. But this thing—this slightly manipulative but well-intentioned ploy—she thought she could get him that far at least. She'd seen heat in his eyes when he watched her, even if he didn't mean for her to see it. He wanted her, and she wasn't above taking advantage.

Though apparently not this night.

One step at a time. Half step, when necessary. It was how she'd gotten what she wanted, what she needed, all of her life.

So he wanted her but didn't want to want her. She'd get him over it.

Seffie wrapped her arms around herself again and looked at the floor for a minute before lifting her gaze to Canaan. She spoke in a small, quiet voice. "Okay, then. It was just a thought."

He was cursing before she even reached the door. He met her there, and placed a soft hand on her arm. "I'm sorry, Sef. That's not the way. If there's something else I can do—"

She wouldn't meet his gaze, just shook her head. But he waited, not letting go of her arm. Slowly, she lifted her head to look at him. "Would you be willing to teach tai chi to me?"

He searched her eyes, likely wondering a little if he was being played. Seffie knew how to look innocent. After a moment, he let go of her arm and stepped back. But he said the words she waited to hear. "Yeah. I could do that."

She nodded, holding back her smile. "Next week, if you have time. I have the week off, and Marta promised me pie-baking lessons. So I'll be here."

He was slow to answer, still a little suspicious. Or simply reluctant. "Yeah, that would work."

CHAPTER TWO

Canaan spent the weekend trying not to look forward to seeing Josefina again. He spent every night suppressing the thought of her crazy, sicko proposal. But he couldn't keep himself from imagining how it would feel to have her in his bed, his arms. To have his body inside hers. He went to sleep each night with a boner and woke up with it, too. Finally, he took to handling the problem himself before he slept. But that didn't change the condition he was in when he woke.

Luckily, the farm was busy. Joss and Marta raised milk goats. Well, mostly it was Joss. Marta was an accountant and she worked several hours a day in her home office. She was also a damn fine cook and baker. She spent a lot of time in the kitchen and taking care of the house.

Joss was the farmer, though the pair had come to the farm through Marta's family. Marta had grown up there, and the couple had come back to live and work when Vermont had become one of the first states where they could get married. Marta's folks were retiring to Florida by that time.

The goats were a pain in the ass, to Canaan's mind. Most of the does only gave good milk in the handful of months after they'd born their kids. So you had to deal with the birthing and the weaning—that's where they were now, in June—and then having a bunch of rowdy babies around who were cute but essentially useless and had to be bottle fed by hand to boot. It went without saying that Marta and Joss would never think about putting them down, so they farmed them out over the course of the summer. They sold most of the females—goat dairies were getting to be big business up in Canada—and gave others away. Marta was pretty good at convincing the local community that goats made good pets. And they were herd animals—they all needed to have a goat buddy or two, so nobody should take just one. She made a big deal of convincing the human kids she knew which of the goats were siblings, and how they shouldn't be separated.

Of course, they were *all* half-sibs. He'd seen to that himself this year, taking over from Joss the physically demanding job of artificial insemination. He told the dams it wasn't fun for him either, and he didn't even want to think about how the semen they'd purchased had been collected.

When the milkers freshened—when they were actively producing milk—they needed to be milked twice a day, which any dairy farmer could tell you was a serious bitch. Pretty much anyone could find something better to do at the butt-crack of dawn.

Still, they'd saved him—Marta and Joss and the fucking goats.

He hadn't mustered out gracefully. His re-entry into civilian life had been pretty ugly. He knew the stats, had seen it coming, and even then he hadn't been able to stop it.

The transition was known to be difficult for those who'd suffered physical and/or emotional trauma. Like having half your buddies die and your own foot blown off by an IED. Check, and check again. It could be tempered, made easier, by a good marriage or solid religious beliefs. No check. And again, no check.

So it was predictable, maybe even inevitable, that he'd fallen into a dark well of anger and misery.

He'd looked like a bum, hitching back from Montreal where he'd spent a month drinking with a guy from the Canadian Forces who'd fought alongside him in Kandahar. He and Labelle weren't doing anything but getting each other drunk and depressed, so Canaan had finally broken free. He was traveling through Vermont, going nowhere that he knew of. He had his grimy thumb out and, beating all, a couple of lesbians stopped and picked him up.

While he smelled up the back seat of their minivan, and without even asking if he was a vet, they thanked him for his service.

He grunted and said he hadn't come home believing in the mission—yet another no check. They said they didn't believe in it either, but he had their gratitude nonetheless.

They took him to the farm and fed him, and that one hot meal was seduction.

He slept with the goats that night, and the next.

The crazy women left their door open and said he could come in for any meal he wanted.

Of all things, it was that he couldn't resist.

The goats were birthing and Joss was busting ass, up all night sometimes making sure all the dams were doing okay. After a while, Canaan couldn't just keep watching her, so he got up, too. It wasn't like he was sleeping anyway. A few days after he proved to be at least semi-trustworthy, Joss stayed in bed.

Then she told him to clean out a small storage room off the milking parlor. Joss bought him a bed, but Marta made it up with clean, soft cotton sheets. More seduction.

Marta fed him and would have mothered him to death. Joss made him find his manhood again. She wanted to rotate her herd in grazing pastures and needed a new one built. She was tough and knew how to dig fencepost holes, but he couldn't stand watching it. So he built the fence, helped with the weaning, and then took over the morning milking.

He couldn't go into that tidy, frilly little farmhouse for a meal without being decently clean. So he started showering off in the barn and washed his clothes by hand one night. The next day there was some cash on his bed—his wages, Joss said. She told him he could use the beat-up farm truck if he needed to drive somewhere, and she left the keys with him.

So, as she'd obviously expected but not instructed him to do, he'd bought work clothes and boots, razors, and deodorant.

A couple weeks later, she told him it would be easier to handle his pay if he had a bank account. So he'd told her his last name and dug out his ID for the local bank and got back on the grid.

He made a little home in that corner of the barn. He started buying food and making most of his own meals. The seduction of that kitchen—spectacular food, warm and steady support, a feeling of belonging, of family—was something he could savor but didn't want to wallow in.

He had to find himself.

Eventually, he started practicing tai chi again, and then the *bō* staff. He'd learned the martial arts from his best friend in boot camp, a guy named Casey who'd been born to a couple of new age hippie parents. Learn to fight, yeah, that was fine. Ranger training, all good. But know the self. Discipline the mind and body. Be aware at every moment, mind, body, spirit.

It entertained the goats. They actually seemed to like him. Each spring, a bunch of the kids would start to follow him around.

He liked them, too, except for that whole pain in the ass deal. They were bright and full of fun and life—and simple. He'd come to like simple. To need it.

Finally, he started writing again, too, a thing he'd done from high school on until his life went to hell in Afghanistan. He bought a guitar and picked a little, whittling out the tunes to match the verses, country songs that were the music he'd grown up on.

Joss would laugh when she finished the evening milking and found him strumming and writing, leaning back on a pile of hay, with half a dozen kids asleep around him, nudging their stupid-cute faces into his pant legs, chewing on denim like as not.

For a while the farm had been his salvation—his place of safety, his hideout. These days, it was his home and the place where his family—the best family he had—lived.

And now it was under attack. By her of the hot little body.

On Monday, in what he figured was a decent tactical move, she brought Tino with her. Canaan was back to eating most of his meals at the house again. There'd come a point when eating by himself in the barn had begun to seem less necessary to his fledgling sense of self and more just plain stupid. So he left the job of reseeding the south pasture to have lunch.

Marta and Josefina were elbow deep in pastry. There were home-fried sweet potato chips and makings for sandwiches on the table, where Tino and Joss were already helping themselves. Canaan said hello when he came in, and all heads turned.

Like the goats, Tino was simple. He was a happy kid, and game, and always sure of his welcome. Really, very much like the goats. He hollered out Canaan's name and ran and leapt. He was seven now, more of an armful than when Canaan had first met him a couple years ago, but still pure in his affection. So Canaan did his job and lifted the boy up for a hug and a kiss.

It was a sweet moment, bringing back a distant memory as happened once in a while on the farm. The slap of the screen door out on the porch. The cranky whine of the aluminum windmill. Women with aprons working in the kitchen. Ruffled curtains and padded chairs to match. Flowers from the garden in a Mason jar.

And a kid who would be welcome everywhere—the kitchen, the barns, the fields—and watched out for, looked after. Be fed scraps of dough. Have hair tousled by weathered hands. For a brief moment, he could remember being that kid, and it was almost enough to bring tears.

Only Josefina was aware. Joss gave him a welcoming nod and Marta, hands busy, sent him the smile that always made him feel the embrace of her heart.

But Josefina watched, and he was sure she could see what that armful of kid did to him. She shouldn't have any way of knowing, but damned if she didn't.

Decent tactic indeed.

Tino liked to talk, so by the time Canaan had nudged between the pie-makers to wash his hands and then sat down at the table, he knew that Leet was taking Tino's brother Jace off to football camp and that baby Rachel was home with Sadie, but would be coming to the farm if one of Sadie's women decided to have a baby that day.

And that the red pepper slices were okay in a sandwich, but it might be better to avoid the "sparegus."

And that Leet said baking pies was one of the five essential qualities in a woman.

Canaan eyed Seffie while he listened to the boy. "Yeah? What are the other four?"

"What other four?"

"Qualities. Essential ones. For a woman."

It took Tino a minute, and then he was perplexed. "I dunno." He said it like it didn't sit well with him that there was something his dad knew that he hadn't shared.

Apparently, that was an offense in the world of Tino.

Canaan carefully met Seffie's eyes and gave her a nod of thanks as she set a glass of iced tea in front of him. Apparently, that was a thing she'd seen Marta do.

He ate like he had work to do—and he did, *dammit*—listening to Tino ramble and talking through a couple farm issues with Joss. Sef and Marta were all about the pies, their attention on the apples they were peeling and slicing.

But not *all* of their attention. He was putting his and Tino's dishes in the washer, thinking he might make a clean getaway, when Seffie spoke.

"How about in an hour and a half or so?"

Canaan straightened and looked at her. She was closer than he'd thought, *bugger it all*. He waited, still flummoxed.

"For a lesson?"

"Oh. Yeah. That'd be fine. On my front porch then. You too, Teen." Because two could play that game.

Tino looked up from his ice cream in question, but Canaan beat feet and left the kid's mother to deal with it.

He knew tactics, too. He'd been a Ranger, man.

But he had to work a bit to convince himself he wasn't on the run, and he was entirely aware of the amused look on Joss's face as she watched him turn tail.

Marta liked to hum while she worked, and right now, she hummed and smiled. She leaned in a little, rubbing shoulders with Josefina, who was slicing the apples Marta had peeled.

"A little thicker. You want them to still have some texture after the pie bakes. He won't think he's worthy of you, you know. He's going to try to resist you."

Josefina adjusted the slices she was making, but paused to look up at Marta. The older woman had been a volleyball player and then a coach—she was about the same height as Canaan. But her brown eyes were warm as she gazed down into Josefina's.

Marta cared a lot about Canaan—probably loved him—so Josefina had to know. "Do you think *I'm* worthy of *him*?"

Marta's hands stilled also. She was a gentle, motherly woman, but she could be counted on to speak the truth. She took a little time answering. "I think the world of Canaan, Josefina. Honestly, I wouldn't say this of many women. But, yes, I think you might be good for him."

"I'm glad you think so. I believe it in my heart, but he's

very stubborn." She'd offered herself to him, and he'd appeared to have no trouble turning her down.

Marta nudged her elbow as she went back to work on the pile of apples. "My money's on you, dear."

Josefina smiled, made hopeful by Marta's approval and confidence.

She had Tino by the hand later, when the pies had baked to perfection and sat cooling on the kitchen table. As they walked to the A-frame, Canaan came out of the barn and headed in the same direction, as though he'd been watching for them. When they met at the steps of his porch, he motioned them up.

"Can we learn stick fighting instead?" Tino asked. "I want to. It's more fun."

Fun. That might be one word for it. They'd both seen Canaan practice in the barn, and it was nothing short of magnificent.

The *bō* staff was six feet long, and, thrust or swung, it could be used as an offensive weapon. But it also served as a defensive weapon. The Japanese monks and peasants who developed the art of *bō* staff fighting were able to twirl it so fast that it functioned as a shield against arrows. Or so she'd learned when she'd studied up after seeing Canaan train.

It was a thing of beauty, watching Canaan work out with the staff. He roamed the barn with it, jabbing and thwacking at targets he'd built onto posts—padded forms that were the shape of a man's torso. He'd twirl it, spinning it with such speed that it became a blur, actually taking on the appearance of a shield. Digging one end into the earth, he'd use it as a pole, making incredible vaults off barn posts and over hay bales. And goats. Always over and around goats, for they seemed to enjoy watching his workouts, too.

To a seven-year-old boy, it was awesome.

To a twenty-two–year-old woman, it was awesome and incredibly hot.

Canaan tousled Tino's hair. "When you were a baby, did you crawl before you walked, walk before you ran?"

Tino, not always a fan of logic, frowned. "Prob'ly," he admitted, at the same time Sef said, "Yes."

Canaan chuckled. "You work on tai chi for a year, and I will teach you *bō* fighting. Deal?"

Tino looked up at her. "How long is a year, Mom?"

Seffie smiled. Sadie had been mother to him for further back than he could remember—before he crawled or walked or ran. But Sadie had always kept Seffie in Tino's life, making regular trips into New York so they could have time together. In his open, affectionate way, Tino had simply accepted that he had two mothers. Just like Sadie did.

Mother and son had become closer since Seffie had moved to the area and was able to see him more frequently. Still, she never tired of hearing him call her "Mom."

"A little less than a year ago, you started first grade, remember? You had Mrs. Miller for your teacher and you sat next to Jaden. You started in the fall, then we had Halloween and then Christmas, and then it got warm and the kids came and you got to watch them get born in the barn. And now it's summer and school's out. All of that is one year."

"That's a long time."

Canaan had been watching them. He put a hand on Tino's shoulder and squatted down so they were eye to eye. "In the life of a boy, yes, it is. But in the life of a man, it is not."

Tino frowned again, but couldn't resist being thought of as a man. "All right."

Canaan smiled and patted Tino's shoulder once. "Good." He stood and directed them to the far end of the porch, facing the windows.

Seffie was aware she was looking into Canaan's bedroom. It was spare now, compared to how it had looked when Sadie lived there. Most of the furniture was gone, and all of the fripperies. There was the bed, covered now with only plain white sheets and a folded blanket. One pillow sat squarely at its head—there were no throw pillows or other decorative touches. The maple dressers were similarly unadorned. It seemed a combination of military precision and Zen.

The *bō* staff was there, next to his bed. For protection, she imagined. At night, when he would feel most vulnerable. And probably for use as a crutch, if he got up during the night without his prosthesis. Which she assumed he had, but had never seen.

It was an intimate moment, looking into his room like that, gazing at the bed where he slept, wishing to be there with him. Making love, yes, but also just lying there with him, sleeping, touching.

"Pay attention." Canaan had to move in front of her, blocking that window into his private life, before she heard him. She realized he'd been speaking, that Tino was already in the stance Canaan wanted.

He paused, startled a little when Seffie turned her gaze to him. She knew he'd understood in that moment what she'd been seeing, imagining. His eyes flared, heated in some way that she was afraid to over-interpret.

"Like Tino," he said, sounding a touch annoyed. "Spread your feet a bit. Bend your knees a little." He demonstrated and she mirrored his position.

He nodded. "Plant your feet. Imagine they're growing roots, sinking deep down into the ground. Like you're anchored there, a part of the earth." Taking a step back, he spoke to both of them now. "Feel the air on your skin. Imagine its substance, know its warmth. Imagine you're a tree, growing up into the sky, seeking the sun, almost reaching it." He was quiet for a moment. "Breathe," he said then. "Deep down into your belly." Crouching in front of Tino, he put his hand low on Tino's abdomen. He poked in a little. "This is your *dantien*, deep inside. It's where you store your chi. You'll use that when you fight. Breathe in down to there." He stood again, facing them both, but he didn't touch Seffie the way he had Tino. "Imagine taking your breath all the way there, and bringing energy in with it. Then breathe out, letting the energy flow out of you, back into the earth, into the sky."

He stood before them, breathing in that solid, centered way. Seffie matched her breath to his and heard Tino do the same.

"Hear your breath. Feel it. Low down in your belly. Put all of your consciousness there. Your thoughts, Tino. Stop thinking and let all of your being focus on your breath."

They continued that for several minutes, with Canaan occasionally speaking, giving pointers and reminders, encouraging. "Now, let your hands rise. Imagine they are as light as the air, as though you have helium balloons attached, lifting them up into the air. Now push them down, as though you were pushing through water."

With a quiet, patient voice, he led them through three forms, movements that were measured and slow but that had martial arts applications. He repeated each one several times before he moved on to the next, always beginning with those first gentle movements of the breath and hands so repetition built memory.

He touched Tino often, adjusting the position of hands or feet or the distribution of weight. But he avoided touching Seffie until, finally, he stepped behind her. He put one hand on her hip, gently pushing her weight forward. The other he placed over her abdomen—at the *dantien*.

"Here," he said. "Feel the energy here. Center your breath here." He stood there, holding her with those gentle, powerful hands, breathing with her.

Seffie tried to open herself to the feel of the energy he described. For long moments her attention was there. Then something changed and she felt a different sort of energy. She was acutely aware of his hands touching her, of the nearness of his chest behind her back, almost close enough to feel.

He was aware of it, too. His breathing changed, and he stepped back, removing the heat of his touch. He took them back to the beginning form once more and brought their session to a close.

"Practice that," he said. "Take a few minutes a couple times a day to practice the forms we've learned. But more important, many moments throughout your day, remember your breathing. You'll want that to be the way you breathe not when you think of it, but all the time."

Seffie nodded formally. "Thank you, Canaan."

He nodded back, silent, watchful, his hands pressed palms together in front of his chest.

"Thank you, Canaan."

Canaan turned his attention to Tino, having a smile for him. "You're welcome, dude. I'll see you at dinner and check your breathing again."

"I'm going to go talk to the goats."

Canaan smiled again. "Sure. You can help me feed a couple of the kids."

Tino ran off to the barn. Canaan looked like he wanted to go with him, but he didn't leave Seffie standing there alone on his porch. She watched him, a little comforted by his apparent unease as they stood there, side by side.

"You're very sweet with him. Thank you." She put a hand on his arm and lifted up. She couldn't—didn't—quite reach his cheek to kiss. Holding there on her toes, she waited until he reluctantly leaned toward her. Suppressing her smile, she touched her lips to his cheek.

Canaan knew that Seffie's hybrid was still parked outside the farmhouse, so he considered staying out in the field and skipping dinner. He'd been fighting a boner ever since he'd put his hands on her and then she'd kissed his cheek out on his front porch. It was only the recollection of Joss's smirk as he'd ducked out of the kitchen after lunch that forced him to clean up and head in. That, and the commitment he'd made to the boy.

Seffie may not be an innocent, but she was too innocent for him. He was barely figuring out how to be a decent friend—and that only because Will, in his patient, looking out for others kind of way, was nudging him along into it. There was simply no way he was ready to be—*ugh*. He couldn't use the word boyfriend, not even in his head. But a man to a woman, a woman's man. He couldn't be that now.

Maybe he wouldn't ever be able to be that. But certainly not now.

And Seffie, for all her ugly history, still had this purity about her—a lot like he saw in her son Tino. He didn't want to sully that, didn't want to take the shine off her.

He wasn't living in the darkness anymore. He was in the light—he *was*. But he wasn't so far from the dark. Sometimes if he turned too fast—just like when he forgot for a moment that his left leg ended in a stump and he lost his balance for a disorienting second—he'd see the shadow of it over his shoulder. Like the darkness was stalking him, no more than a few small paces behind. He was ahead of it and planned to stay that way, worked hard every day to stay that way. But it was still too near a thing to put someone else's life and happiness on the line for the hope of it.

And he wouldn't suck up someone else's light to fend off the darkness in him. It would be too likely a thing that he'd pull her into his dark.

So he told his stupid dick to stand down and went in to dinner.

He'd eat and then help with cleanup, and all of that wouldn't take more than an hour or two. He'd chat with Tino about the goats, and eventually, the kid's mother would have to take him home and she'd be gone and he'd be safe.

Except that Leet came to fetch Tino, showing up just in time for pie like the guy had some kind of radar for it.

Leet was a lot of man. He was big and muscled like a pro quarterback would be, but also damn good-looking, and he oozed the sort of charm that women loved. For sure, he had Joss and, especially, Marta, his two mothers-in-law, wrapped around his little finger.

Regretfully, Canaan couldn't hate him for it. The guy was truly decent. He loved Sadie strongly and faithfully. He'd taken on her two boys like they were his own, becoming a great dad to them and the baby girl Sadie had given him. And there was nothing fake in his regard for the moms. He honestly loved them, letting Marta mother him and Joss give him Monday morning quarterback tips on how to improve his game.

There had been some days when Leet had watched Canaan suspiciously—back when Sadie was still living at the farm and Leet was trying to get into her pants. In those days, he took Canaan's ubiquitous presence as a possible threat. *As if.* But Sadie had fallen for Leet so completely and transparently that it hadn't taken Leet long to get over worrying about it. And then there'd been that deal where Will and Canaan, camouflaged and armed, had mounted a mission to rescue Sadie and Leet from a handful of Middle Eastern thugs. It had ended easily and well, but Leet knew what Canaan had done and been willing to do, and was heartfelt grateful for it.

So he was another friend. Sadie was easier for him, and Will nudged it along in the way that he did, but the fact was that Leet, too, had worked his way past Canaan's shields.

And it was nice to have someone else for Joss to turn her flinty eye to. Canaan had had enough of her watching him squirm every time Josefina had directed her attention to him.

Which was a damn lot. *Damn woman.*

He kicked back and enjoyed watching Leet blush.

"What's that?" Leet asked, in response to Joss's question. Like he hadn't heard her the first time.

"The five essential qualities in a woman. We heard baking pies was one. I wondered about the other four."

"Yeah, Dad."

Leet gave Tino a look, and Canaan figured there'd be talk about the man club on their way home.

"Um, well, there are a lot of important qualities, aren't there?"

"Uh-huh. But the top five?"

Marta smiled serenely, but Seffie raised a brow like she was all interested, too.

"Yeah, let's see. It's been a while since I had that conversation."

Another look to Tino promised retribution.

"Well, I'm sure that having some brains was on the list. And a sense of humor." He had a twinkle in his own eye now. "And then I think it was polite table manners and good penmanship."

Joss snorted.

"Or maybe it was doesn't snort when she laughs."

"Or fart when she sneezes," Tino piped in.

The women all laughed, but Leet nodded seriously at Tino. "That's important, but I wouldn't call it top five." He gave it some thought. "Maybe down around nine or ten." He stood then and lifted Tino onto his hip. "Come on, buddy. Let's go before you get me in any more trouble. Say goodnight to the grams."

Leet walked him around the table, both of them giving hugs and kisses to the women. Seffie took an extra moment, breathing in the scent of her son's hair.

When the two were gone—Leet with his plastic container of leftover pie replacing the empty he'd shamelessly turned in—Canaan said he'd clean up and tried sending the women from the kitchen. Joss and Marta liked to watch the evening news and then a couple game shows.

Two out of three of the women complied. But Sef stayed and started carrying dishes to the sink. He did his best to ignore her, rinsing the dishes and setting them in the second basin before loading the washer. She nudged her way in, though, reaching across him for the spray nozzle.

He felt her touch along his whole length and bristled. He shot her a look, and she acted all innocent.

"What?"

"You're crowding me."

"I did nothing different than if you'd been Joss or Marta."

Huh. Then why were his arm and hip on fire from her touch? "Why don't you go join them? I'll finish these."

Or, more, *why don't you go home*? She had a perfectly fine place to go to, across the river with Leet's folks.

She lifted a brow like she might be offended, and kept a little stink eye on him while she hung the dishtowel. "Fine."

"Yeah. Goodnight."

She didn't answer. He should have had a clue she wasn't done with him.

Canaan worked out hard with the *bō* staff.

Bō staff fighting had a tradition he loved. Japanese peasants and monks had developed it, when the Samurai warriors had forbidden them to have bladed weapons. Like the medieval farmers who used pikes and scythes in battle, it was a matter of making the most of what you had at hand.

And in this case, raising it to an art.

There was a professor of Japanese history down at the college who'd also studied, and Canaan and he got together a couple times a month to spar. They used the gym sometimes, but the two of them had also set up a pretty good fight course in the barn. He had a fine time that night, working out his temper against the sparring dummies and entertaining the goats.

He kept at it until he was drenched in sweat and he'd exhausted his body. He did some tai chi to cool down and then showered off.

He wasn't really fooling himself when he sat out on one of the rockers. He knew perfectly well that Josefina was still in the farmhouse. And he wasn't at all surprised when he heard the slap of the screen door and she came over and up onto his porch.

He *was* a little surprised when she crawled onto his lap. Automatically, his arms came up to hold her, one wrapped around her back, and the other draped along her legs to her hip. He wouldn't be responsible for her falling.

She put her arms around him and rested her head on his shoulder. He rocked a little, holding her like that, until she spoke quietly.

"*This* is me crowding you."

No fuck.

Whatever else she was there for, she was there for comfort. He'd seen how hard it was for her when Leet carried Tino off in his arms. So he took a breath and squeezed her a little closer. Rocked a little more, until she let out that sigh she'd been holding.

He spoke with his lips pressed into her hair. "You couldn't have done better for Tino. You can't go back and make some better decision. There wasn't a better decision to make. Stop pretending there was some other choice. There wasn't. You did the right thing, the only right thing to be done." She fucking had tears wetting his T-shirt. He jiggled her a little. "I mean it. Stop it."

Showing no shame, she rubbed her cheeks against his shirt, drying herself on him. She sniffed a little, then spoke into his chest. "You're right. I know you are. It's just—it's just hard."

"Of course it's hard. If it wasn't hard, it would be easy, and then it wouldn't fucking be life, would it?"

Okay, maybe that piece of nonsense was a little gruff, but she didn't seem to object too much. Still, she sighed again.

"Yes, you're right."

They were quiet for another little bit, and then he felt her lips on his neck. "Stop that, too, dammit."

She did, but of course she would have to talk about it. "Do you know you were the only one who noticed that it made me sad to see him go with Leet?"

He didn't answer. Or maybe he gave her a muffled, "hmm."

"And earlier, at lunch—"

Of course she wasn't done.

"When you held Tino, I was the only one who noticed that it meant something to you. It touched you in some way, didn't it?"

He didn't answer that one at all.

"We know each other, Canaan. We see each other. More than anyone else knows us or sees us."

A quarter moon hung over his shoulder, barely enough light for him to see her. She raised her head and looked back into his eyes. She shouldn't have the light to see, but he knew she did. He knew she was seeing him, just like she said.

And he knew it when she lifted her mouth. He knew she was going to kiss him. And he didn't do anything to stop it.

Her mouth was slightly open and she did nothing more than touch their lips together. She held there, softly touching while they both breathed, sharing the same air.

Then his breath was unsteady and hers was, too. His arms jerked, his brain losing the battle to keep them gentle and still on her. Her arms tightened around his neck and his around her body and then they were close, their bodies hard against each other and their mouths melding.

"Mmm." It was kind of a hum and kind of a moan and he didn't know which of them had made it. But he felt something deep in his chest, hot and loosening all at once, rumbling out.

His tongue was in her mouth and then hers in his, and she tasted so sweet. He sucked on her, suckled, like those damn stupid goat kids, her tongue and her lips. He took her breath, waiting for her to exhale so he could take her in. He took her moans, swallowing them with his mouth.

Her arms were hard around him now, her hands stroking his neck and shoulders, her fingers twining tightly in his hair. Her breasts were against his chest, firm mounds and then the hard points of her nipples he could feel through their clothing. And her hip rocked against him, rolling into the rigid, incredibly sensitive length of his erection.

With the barest thread of control, he gripped hard and steadied her, preventing that movement. Even one more caress from her hip and he wouldn't come back from it.

But this he could do. This kissing, touching, sharing breath. He felt like he could do it forever.

He wouldn't, though. They'd opened their eyes, sunk deep into each other's gazes. They'd softened the touches of their lips then swooped deep again. They'd stroked each other, hair and cheek, jaw and neck, spreading touches and kisses everywhere.

They'd spoken each other's name, roughly, then softly, gently.

It was all he could want for the rest of his life. This would be enough. More than enough.

But he stood. He held her in his arms, their mouths still joined, and stood. He carried her to the steps, and, carefully, left leg descending first, one stair at a time, he took her down. Then he walked with her in his arms to her car.

When he got there, he set her down, letting her body slide down his in a long embrace.

"Go home, Josefina."

"I'm coming back tomorrow."

"I wish you wouldn't."

"No, you don't."

She was wrong. But she was right, too.

"Josefina has a boyfriend."

Will lifted a brow and studied Canaan for a long minute. They were sitting across from each other at the Basin Diner, coffee on the table and their breakfasts coming. Canaan had called Will the night before, after he'd watched Seffie's tail-lights disappear, and set up the meeting. The thing about having a friend was, sometimes, you had someone to go to for help.

Will's wife Kate was a psychotherapist and the man had no trouble channeling her. He enjoyed it, in fact, in a smarmy, obnoxious way. "And how does that make you *feel*, Canaan?"

"Stuff it, Hunter. How I feel is not the point. He's pressuring her to have sex."

Will sat back, serious now. "Define 'pressure.'"

"What does it matter?"

"Well, we presume he's a guy. Guys want to have sex. Is he asking nicely, and backing off when she says no? *Is* she saying no? Is this a problem for her, or for you?"

"You know she has some shit in her past."

"Actually, I don't *know* that."

"Well, she does."

"I believe you."

"I want to make sure she doesn't get hurt."

Will sighed. "Do you really think she can't handle herself?"

"I think she shouldn't have to."

"What is it you think I can do?"

"I want you to check him out. Make sure he's an okay guy."

"You don't want me to confront him, put a little fear of God into him?"

"You'd do that?"

"Hell no."

The dude had pretty good, honorable standards about his job, and he was right to object.

Will sat back while the waitress Marlie set their plates in front of them. The dude was showing signs of living with a woman. He'd ordered an egg white omelet with veggies and wheat toast—hold the home fries and breakfast meat. The man was whipped.

Canaan had showed no such restraint. He was looking at eggs over easy, potatoes, and bacon.

But they both watched Marlie walk away. She was known for the sweet sway to her hips, and Will apparently hadn't lost his manhood to such an extent that he couldn't still appreciate something like that. Marlie had married her high school sweetheart, a burly trucker whom she loved like a big teddy bear. No one ever did more than look.

When she'd refilled their coffees and turned her back on them again, Will went on. "No," he said. "Even just checking him out is a misuse of my star. Why can't you do it? I'm sure you can track this guy as well as I can."

"Yeah. But you won't want to kill him. I might."

Will put his coffee down and sharpened his gaze on Canaan. "That's sounding a little serious."

"It's not."

The deputy raised his brows again.

"It's really not."

"You're privy to her history—and you're the only one I know of who is. You don't want her to get hurt. And you might want to kill the guy she's seeing. Sorry, man, but it sounds serious as a painful little sore on your dick."

"You're a painful little sore on my ass."

Will sighed. "What's the guy's name?"

"Trevor."

Will waited a second. "That's it?"

"You a detective or not?"

"You got anything else? You know when she sees him? Anything?"

"I'll see what I can find out."

$\mathcal{C}$HAPTER THREE

Canaan spent the rest of the week in hell. Well, sometimes it was heaven, but mostly it was hell. Even when it felt like heaven—like those next evenings when he had Seffie in his arms again—later, when he couldn't sleep for the thrumming of his body, he decided that had been hell, too.

He felt like a proud feral wolf being turned into someone's damn lap dog. Like he begged for scraps—food, affection—and then was ashamed of himself for sinking so low as to want them. Crave them.

Josefina came each morning and, if she managed to catch him at breakfast, she gave him a kiss in greeting the same as she did Marta and Joss. Except that she kissed his lips instead of his cheek, and held there for a couple seconds that were laden with unspoken meaning. Joss and Marta went on about their business as though nothing out of the ordinary had happened, while he sat there stunned.

She spent the days acting like she belonged there—Joss and Marta, too, seeming to accept that she was an expected part of life on the farm. She was in the kitchen baking and cooking, then working in the gardens—Marta's flowerbeds and kitchen garden. She tossed feed outside the henhouse and collected eggs. She helped nurse the kids.

And showed up on his porch every afternoon for a lesson.

She'd invaded his space, left him with nowhere to be that hadn't been infused with her essence, her scent. Like a damn dog marking its territory.

It was better on the days she brought Tino—and worse, too. Tino was a good distracter—he took some attention, broke a bit into that intense awareness Canaan always had for Seffie. The boy gave Canaan something to do during the tai chi lesson besides focus on Sef.

But Tino brought out the kid in Seffie, too, making her look cute and sweet and incredibly attractive. She joined him in playing with the goats, looking so much like a kid herself that he felt like a lecher watching her, wanting her. They'd run together and tumble in the hay, and Canaan was reminded of how much she was still a child when her son had been born.

Like kids, the two of them decided the goats needed a playground and initiated a campaign to have Canaan build one. They started with Joss, citing Internet sources that documented happier goats and better milk production when they had play equipment. The pair brought a couple colorful, sturdy balls and got the goats playing a stupid—and sort of cute—kind of soccer.

Before he knew what hit him, Canaan was building a "climbing mountain," moving earth and stacking old tires. The two nuts designed a tree house/pirate ship/play set that had ladders to climb and bells to ring and a couple puzzles to solve that earned the goats a bit of feed.

Like he didn't have real work to do.

But Joss helped and even Marta, and he had to admit he enjoyed building with Tino. There were sweet moments teaching Tino to use simple tools and watching him strut around with the tool belt Seffie had fashioned for him.

And other sweet moments watching Seffie act like a girl. She was bright and capable in dozens of ways, but she couldn't get over swinging a hammer in a totally incompetent girlish way. Canaan was embarrassed by how good it felt when she turned those big blues on him, expecting him to rescue her from some carpentry *faux pas*. "The nail must have been bad," she'd say.

He laughed that week. It took him a few days to recognize it. He knew he'd come to smile more in the years he'd been healing on the farm. And by the time he realized it, it already felt natural—that rumble from deep in his chest, that lightness of heart. The first time he caught himself at it, Seffie was watching him and he understood she'd seen it first. Seeing him, knowing him just like she'd said. Better than any others, better than he did himself.

That next night she was to leave to take Tino home herself. But the two stayed late, having decided to climb to the roof of the barn and watch the stars come out. Marta tut-tutted at the danger until Canaan agreed to take them up there and keep them safe. So they lay together, on a thick blanket protecting them from the rough shingles. By the time it was dark, Seffie had her head on his shoulder and Tino was sacked out between them—a pretty ineffective chaperone.

Seffie rolled more toward Canaan, wrapping one arm across his chest and turning her face to his. Then they were watching each other instead of the stars. He didn't resist when she wrapped her fingers into his hair and brought his mouth close.

They touched only there—her hand in his hair, her head against his shoulder, and their lips. But it was a consuming kiss. It tightened his body and made him moan. He stopped pretending that he was passive about it and took it to her, capturing her mouth, stroking with his tongue, nipping with his teeth. It was a hot turn-on, letting loose the leash he'd held on his passion, knowing that Tino's presence between them would restrain him from going too far.

Though every bit of it was too far and he knew it. Even the softest, most innocent kiss was too much. But he was tired of resisting, of holding himself back from something his soul longed for. And so he took her, took this bit of her he could have. He tasted her, drew her into himself. When she brought her hand to his face, he took that, too, biting the flesh of her thumb, sucking her fingers into his mouth, using his teeth on them.

Seffie was breathing harshly, too, moaning her desire. Passion built to a crescendo, as though they'd consummated more than they had. Rough, hard kisses, secured with fingers clutching, mixed with coarse breaths, came to a kind of climax. Then Canaan pulled back, still holding her to him, their gazes locked as they gasped for breath. He held her there for a long time, until his breath settled and the tension of his muscles loosened. Gently, he let her down, resting her head on his arm, foreheads touching.

She kept a hand at his neck and he knew she was feeling the gradual slowing of his pulse. Most of an hour passed before he slipped his arm out from under her, lifted Tino against his shoulder, and took her down off the roof.

The next day, Wednesday, Sadie came in the afternoon. She stayed and played a bit, mostly laughing at the amateur carpenters—and with them, as Canaan forced a hammer into her hand, too. Then she took Tino home. Josefina spent the evening in the farmhouse—she and Marta were finishing up a batch of goat cheese. Canaan worked out in the barn and then waited for her on his porch, not pretending otherwise even to himself.

It was dark when she came, nearly moonless now. But she walked right up to him as though it was daylight, directly opposite of the way being around her seemed to blind him. And she took to his lap again, only this time straddling him and bringing her mouth to his without hesitation.

He was hard immediately. Well, the truth was, he'd been aching for her the whole last hour, while he'd been watching her move around inside the brightly lit kitchen. But she rubbed up against him, bringing her center hard to his erection, and he knew there was no secret about his aroused state.

It didn't seem to put her off. Her mouth was warm and wet, eager against his. And she rocked her pelvis, lighting a fire that was hotly consuming. He gripped her hips, steadying her but not exactly pushing her away. Running on primitive instinct, he arched up against her.

She didn't object to that either. She wrapped her arms around his shoulders and sank her breasts into his chest. He helped her out, tightening one arm around her hips and bringing the other behind her back, using it to press her breasts more firmly against him.

Their mouths mated while their bodies strained against each other. He gripped her harder, a breath away from an embarrassing adolescent loss of control when he tore his mouth away from hers.

"Don't move. I fucking mean it, Sef. Don't move."

She was as close to orgasm as he was—he could tell even if she couldn't. He threw his head back and huffed out uneasy breaths, afraid even that much movement would end it for him. In a bit, the rush in his ears calmed enough that he could hear Sef saying his name in a needy, uncertain voice, like she didn't know what was happening. Like she needed him to do something for her.

Which she did, but it wasn't what she thought. She needed him to be adult and responsible, a better man than maybe he was.

He inched his raging hard-on away from her incredibly tempting heat. She moaned and he brought her head against his chest. He pressed his lips into her hair.

"Go home, baby. Please, go home."

"No, Canaan."

"Yes. Please, yes, baby."

She hung her head in a way that made him feel like a lowlife, but she pulled herself back, stood, and walked away.

The next day she didn't come until afternoon. She brought Tino with her and followed his instructions through their tai chi lesson without making much eye contact. That evening, she took Tino and left before dinner.

On Friday, it rained. Canaan hauled feed from the farm supply store in the village and took that as an opportunity to skip lunch at the house. He'd seen Seffie's car there early and didn't mind having a decent excuse to avoid her. So he sat in the diner and watched Marlie's ass some more, but she wasn't the one he was thinking about.

He went in for dinner, though, and ate with the three women—Seffie was there, but Tino had spent the day home with Sadie, he learned—and excused himself as soon as he could. Then he went and sat in the dark inside his house, picking out a new tune on his guitar.

Nothing like a little woman blues to bring out the country in a man.

His front porch didn't have an overhang, so when she knocked on his door, he either had to leave her out there in the rain or go let her in. He didn't exactly open the door with a big welcome. He stood in the opening, his hand latched firmly on the doorknob, and looked at her.

She looked back, not appearing at all distressed to be standing there with water dampening the thin little top she wore and sending her hair into wild coils. She knew, as he did, what would happen if he stepped back and let her in.

It was left up to him. He got the sense she'd stand there as long as she needed to. Like maybe she'd still be there in the morning.

He was past being able to do the right thing. There was no doubt he was opening himself up for a world of hurt—and maybe her, too. Despite that patient, expectant look on her face, somewhere deep inside was a wounded and scared little girl.

He wanted her.

She wanted someone else, and came with baggage like

Lady Gaga on a world tour to boot.

Screwed. He was fucking screwed.

If she had any sense at all, she'd turn and run.

"You should have gentle and careful." He said it roughly, abruptly, and she startled just a little. "I'm not sure I can give you that."

"I'm not afraid of you."

She fucking should be, and he knew it, if she didn't. Still, being the better part of an idiot, he stepped back. Like a lamb to slaughter, she walked through. He shut the door behind her and looked down at her.

"Do you know my left leg ends in a stump?"

Abrupt as it was, that one didn't make her blink. "Yes."

"Who told you?" Not many people knew, and he didn't think they were talkers.

"I know you served in Afghanistan. When you dance, you very deliberately turn on your left foot as often as your right, except after you've had two drinks, and then you seem to forget. That appears to be your limit—two drinks. When you train, in the barn, with your staff, you practice a new move more on your left than on your right—almost three times as much."

He lifted a brow.

"In medical school, we're trained to be acute observers."

He nodded. "I guess."

And like a woman, she wasn't done.

"When you carry me down a set of steps, you take them one at a time, leading with your left. The same when you carry Tino down a ladder. That's the only time you favor your left side."

When the burden he carried mattered more than the pride he took in managing his disability. The fucking bitch saw everything. *Dammit*. Now *he* was scared.

She looked up at him. "Is that part of why you don't think you should be with me?"

That pissed him off, and he didn't exactly hold back. "No. And you don't want me to be with you, remember? You just want me to f—"

She didn't like the word he was about to use, so she stopped him with her fingers against his lips. And gave him a little glare.

He glared back, until she lifted her fingers.

—"*you*, so you can go have fun with your boyfriend."

She frowned and used those blue eyes on him like she was *acutely observing* the dark corners of his soul. She changed her mind a couple times before she finally spoke. "I want to be with you now. That's what I want, Canaan."

Lifting a hand into the hair at the nape of her neck, he brought her closer and pressed his lips against the top of her head. "I don't want to hurt you."

She put her hand at his shoulder and pushed back against him enough that she could look up at him. "You won't. I know you won't."

He stood looking at her, wishing he could find a way to tell her no. Then she went up on tiptoe to reach his lips with hers.

He bent the littlest bit, keeping his eyes open, like that could protect him from the heartache that was coming. But then she touched him, and he got her taste, and it was over for him.

Wrapping his arms hard around her, he brought her close and devoured. He opened her mouth with his and delved in. On this, at least, he didn't have to hold back. They'd spent enough time with their lips locked together, out on the porch and up on the barn roof, that he didn't need to worry about her. Not yet.

He snugged her up close so his erection was nestled into her lower belly. She rocked against him like she liked it, like she knew what was coming and it didn't worry her at all.

Probably, though, she wouldn't be expecting him to shuck her right out of her hot little cut-off jeans and take her up against the door. So before he totally lost his grip, he pulled back.

His breath was already rough and unsteady, but so was hers. He looked at her as he got a little distance, and she looked back, while he grasped for a thread of control. Finally, he stepped back, took her hand, and walked them to the bedroom.

Canaan's room was dark. The yard light outside cast shadows through the rain-drenched windows that formed nearly two full walls. The white sheets on the bed appeared a cool gray. They were already neatly folded back. The bedside table held a reading lamp, a single book, and one condom.

He took her to the bed then turned and faced her. He touched her softly, stroking her face, her arms. He leaned in so he cocooned her in the warmth of his breath.

"If there's anything you don't like, Josefina, anything you don't want, you say so."

He assumed she was afraid. Seffie knew she should be. She understood now, though it had taken years, that what had happened to her in the past was childhood sexual abuse.

But she hadn't felt like a child when Mateo, her mother's on-again, off-again boyfriend, had put his hands on her. Had forced himself *into* her. She hadn't felt like a child ever again.

It hadn't seemed like abuse, but like...her own bad luck.

And it didn't appear to relate at all to what happened when she was in Canaan's arms. From the first moment she'd seen him, she'd recognized that she would be safe with him. She *knew*, like she knew the color of her eyes, that he wouldn't hurt her.

She was quite certain he was more afraid than she was.

She breathed in his scent, her face burrowed into the nook of his shoulder, and touched her fingers to his face. "I know you won't hurt me. I trust you."

He sighed once, then arched back and tore his T-shirt over his head. When he leaned back over her, where she touched him now was hot skin. He stood still, not quite suppressing a fine tremor, while she learned him.

He'd had more wounds than the loss of part of his leg. Surgical scars marked him, over his left clavicle and below his ribs on his right flank. And jagged, puckered remnants of traumatic injuries.

But still, he was beautiful. His chest was muscled, smooth. The skin was tanned and tight over his lean torso. His flat nipples were dark, almost black. Coarse hairs peeped from his underarms.

She touched and tasted and nuzzled, breathing him in. She used her palms and fingers, her lips and tongue.

Seffie knew he was hard. She'd felt it earlier when he'd held her so close. And she could see it now, bulging down where the whiter skin below his tan line disappeared into the low-slung waist of his jeans.

He shuddered under her gaze and she looked up into the nearly black depths of his eyes. Watching him, she leaned back and put her fingers to the top button of her cotton blouse.

His gaze was hot on her. It flared when she opened the first button, and again with the next. He growled as the third one let go and her blouse separated enough to reveal the curves of her breasts. Grasping her hips with his big strong hands, he steadied her. Or himself.

"Keep going."

He said it roughly, curtly, like he didn't care anymore whether she was afraid. Then even that wasn't enough and he did it himself, tearing open the last buttons and pushing the blouse down her arms and off. He took her hips again and dropped his head so his forehead ground into her sternum. She could feel his hot breath on her breasts.

"You're so beautiful, Seffie. Fucking beautiful."

He nuzzled and kissed, then ran his tongue along—and just under—the lacy edge of her bra. Growling again, he wrapped his arms around her and brought her close against him. Raising his head, he took her mouth again and lifted to lay her down on the bed. He came with her, reaching down to slide her sandals off and doing the same with his shoes. Then he was beside her, partially over her. One thigh secured both of hers and he leaned on one elbow, his big shoulders looming over her.

Watching her, he rested one hand above her breast, over her heart. He left it there a long moment before he followed the side of her bra around to the back. She arched up a little while he used skilled fingers to release the fastening.

He brought his hand back, leaving the bra in place. Then he grasped a strap at her shoulder and slowly tugged it down.

It was a certain kind of torture. He bared her a little at a time. And he kept tension in his hold on the fabric, so it scraped against her skin as he moved it. He paused when it caught against her nipple. It was hard, distended, and acted as an impediment.

Seffie huffed out a breath when he tugged and the nipple released. Canaan murmured out a breath, too, closing his eyes for a moment in apparent wonder. He lifted up off his elbow then, bringing the bra out from her other arm and peeling it away.

When he came back, he put one hand over her breast and his lips over her mouth. He kissed her softly as he palmed her breast, a gentle motion that stimulated the nipple. His hand clasped, massaging, and then his thumb and finger took hold of that tight peak. He lifted his head to watch as he softly rolled it between his fingers.

Seffie's breath caught and she arched, that touch on her nipple sending a thrill of excitement shivering through her body. Canaan pinched a little harder and put his lips at her neck, near her ear.

"You like that, don't you?"

"Yes. Canaan."

His name was a little whimper from her lips.

"You'll like this, too."

His fingers kept toying with her while he lowered his mouth to her other breast. He covered her, the hot, wet grasp of his mouth a wicked possession. She could feel his tongue sliding over her nipple, subtly stirring. Then, abruptly, he sucked hard on her, drawing her deep into his mouth, the strong tension prickling her nipple.

"Aahh." Seffie cried out, her body jerking, bowing up, offering itself. She felt taken, consumed by him.

Driven witless, she tossed her head. She didn't have a thought about what had happened to her in her past, but only of what this moment felt like, the incredible sexual awakening of her body, the sweet, hot sensations generated by Canaan's mouth and fingers.

And by him, merely his presence—his hot body alongside hers, his focus, his obvious determination to give her this indescribable pleasure.

He kept at it, squeezing her, pulling hard with his mouth, until her body was rocking with need, until her breath came in huffs and she chanted his name, demanding—more. He lifted over her, working her moist nipple now with his thumb, and watched her face while he slid his other hand down her belly. He stroked her bare midriff, then inched lower, slowly, over her denim shorts.

He touched her there, at the juncture of her thighs, right at that hot, needy center. Only a touch, the barest pressure, as he watched her.

"Canaan!" She wanted to tell him to move, to press, to *do more*, but she didn't have the words, didn't have her brain about her enough to form a complete thought. "Canaan!"

He only watched her, his eyes intense and glittering. Finally, in frustration, she flexed her hips, digging in with her heels and nudging herself up against her fingers.

Knowing satisfaction suffused his gaze then and he gave her a little—just a little—of what she wanted. He stroked his fingers down the seam of her shorts, a gentle rub of that exquisitely sensitive spot.

"Oh. More. Oh. Oh. More."

He was going to kill her. She needed, *needed*, and he did nothing but keep up that too little, not nearly enough touch.

"Canaan!" In her mind, she was cursing—aggravated, needy commands. Finally, in frustration, she tore at the fly of her shorts, opening them and lifting to slide them down and off. "Touch me! I need—I need..."

He came hard over her, his knee pressing her thighs open, his mouth taking hers. Then he did what she wanted, what she needed. He stroked her, magic fingers knowing exactly how to touch, how to—*drive* her. In moments, she was bucking, tearing her mouth free of his so she could draw a harsh breath, so she could cry out. She arched up off the bed into his body, shuddering, seeking.

Fast then, furiously, he rubbed her.

And she screamed.

Canaan halted every motion with that wild sound. Maybe she was a screamer, and he'd love that. But he couldn't be certain there wasn't some fear in it.

He didn't object to a little moment of panic when he had a woman in his bed. A bit of thunderstruck, fear of the god Canaan was really a fine thing. He took a moment to remember that cocky feeling, and how long it had been since he'd known it. But the here and now called.

He knew something about flashbacks, and he knew it was possible Seffie had gone to some bad situation and time in her head. And if she had, his fingers were in a totally inappropriate place.

She'd had a hard orgasm. There was no doubt about that. Her body still thrummed with it, her breath was still rough and agitated. She had one hand tangled in her hair, her face turned away from his. With her other, she had an iron grip on his wrist, though whether that was a good or bad thing he didn't know.

He needed something from her, some sign. A smile or a couple words conveying her undying gratitude.

His dick was entirely sure she was happy. It was thinking, *game on*.

But he had the sense to know his dick didn't always know everything.

He pressed his lips to her shoulder, then lifted up to look at her carefully. What he could see of her. "Sef? Are you okay?"

She didn't turn, but she opened her eyes. He just barely caught it, with that gorgeous hair tousled and half-covering her face. "Mmm."

Which sounded good, but—"I don't know what that means."

"I'm okay, Canaan. Very, very okay."

"You screamed."

She turned her face then to look at him, and he knew she'd recognized his worry. "It wasn't a bad kind of scream."

She was so fucking beautiful, those blue eyes behind that shiny dark red hair, those long lashes. Looking at him like he was indeed the god Canaan. He recognized the look now, and couldn't hold back his grin. "It was a good scream?"

She smiled.

Oh, yeah.

"I wonder if you've noticed where my fingers are." Inside her, where she was so hot and tight it made his eyeballs want to roll back into his head.

She let go of that firm grip she had on his wrist. She put her hand over his, pressing down. And while she did that, she rocked up a little, taking more of him inside. "I noticed."

Somehow, she squeezed his fingers.

"Sweet Jesus. Sef."

He ducked his head and rolled a bit so he could press his hard-on into the mattress rather than into her. Grasping for control, he shuddered out a breath. When he thought he had a handle on it again, he looked up at her. "More?"

She nodded.

He kissed her—gratitude, encouragement, promise. Then kissed her again, lower. And lower.

He played at her belly button, nipping and tonguing her. Then lower still, nearly to where his fingers had found heaven.

She was shaved bare, pretty as a—peach. Her little pink bud peeked out in invitation.

He didn't turn it down. He took her with his mouth, sucking gently and then stroking, probing with his tongue. It only took a couple minutes to warm her to it, and then she was humming again, rocking again. The grip on his fingers loosened a little and he stimulated her there, too, pushing in and out of that sweet heat.

He teased her some, driving her high, close, then backing off a bit, letting her hover.

She wasn't only a screamer, but a talker, too, and he loved that every bit as much. She told him what she liked and how it felt, and bitched at him the last time he left her hanging. He let her have what she wanted then, what she needed, and she cried out again when he took her over.

It was pure pleasure this time, knowing she was getting off, sure that he wasn't scaring her.

So he was surprised when she complained, almost before she was done screaming.

"That wasn't what I wanted."

He put his lips alongside the crest of her hipbone and sucked—hard, leaving a mark. Trying not to think about his intent there.

"Oh, that was what you wanted."

"Not *all* of what I wanted. Canaan."

She waited for him to lift his head and look at her. He didn't want to. He'd have been happy to stop right there. To let her know that she could find pleasure in sex, that she didn't have to be afraid.

He couldn't give her more without putting his own heart at risk. But he knew he wouldn't say no to whatever she asked.

She touched his face, her fingers soft and sweet and heartbreaking. "You know what I want."

He grasped her fingers and held them to his mouth, taking them in. "Are you sure, baby?"

"Yes. Please."

It was going to kill him. Softly kill him.

Seffie knew he was reluctant.

She knew he'd held back so far. Knew that he could pleasure her, plumb the secrets of her body, and still not give himself to her. He could grant the favor she'd asked. He could accept her trust, take her in his gentle hands, and show her the delights of lovemaking.

And still hold himself removed. Give pleasure and watch her accept it, but not give himself.

She knew that was what he'd prefer, and she couldn't let him have it.

She wanted him. All of him. Not just his very significant ability to give her pleasure. She couldn't let him hold himself back. She needed him to be there with her.

Sure, it was a little scary to think of him breaching her, penetrating, as she knew would come next. She'd felt the size of him before he'd moved and pressed himself into the bed rather than into her thigh.

But she didn't want half measures. She didn't want her heart involved while he held back.

So she waited, eyes wide open, while he studied her. After a long moment, he rolled over onto his back. Lying next to her, he unfastened his jeans and shimmied them down his thighs. Keeping an eye on her, he reached over for the condom, opened it, and peeled it down to cover himself. When he rolled back, she could feel the pressure of his erection again. Hot this time, with only the thin layer of latex dividing them.

He held over her and tangled the fingers of one hand in her hair. Reeling it in, he used it to secure her head. Sinking down over her, he kissed her softly, sweetly. Then he moved and centered himself between her legs.

Kissing her again, he watched her eyes. "Tell me to stop. Now. In a minute. Any time."

"I won't. I want this, Canaan. I already like the way you feel."

He'd moved barely close enough that she could discern

the pressure of him at her opening. He felt big and threatening and compelling. She met his eyes, waiting, daring, but still, she knew there was a little shudder in her breath.

Her body gave way as he pressed in a little, a stretching sensation that bordered on painful. "Keep going."

"I'm afraid I'm a little big for you, honey."

"Don't stop." She might have sounded a touch frantic there, but he did what she asked.

With a fierceness in his eyes, he sank in, fully, deeply. "Ah."

His body was rigid with the control he exerted. He'd dropped his head, nudging into the crook of her neck. "'Ah'?"

Seffie wasn't sure what she'd meant either. It shouldn't have been physically possible for her body to accommodate him. A "little big" in no way did justice to his size. She was filled impossibly, improbably, stretched and taut.

It should have hurt. It should have paralyzed her with fear. But it felt good, so taking, so owning. And hot, too, so very stimulating.

It was amazing, really, that this thing that could be used to hurt, to punish, to *master*, could be so powerfully moving and so wickedly stimulating.

"Canaan. Canaan, you're—*inside* me. It feels so good. So good." It did. It really did. But he just held there, filling her, stretching her, and shouldn't there be...

He moved once, sliding out, making her moan with the loss of it, and then croon when he filled her again. "Oh. Umm. That's good."

"Good, Seffie? You want more of that?"

"Yes, Canaan. More. A lot more."

"Sweetheart, I'm afraid..."

"More, Canaan." *Dammit*. She didn't think she said the word out loud, but he might have got the intent.

He lifted over her on his elbows, watching her face. He managed to get his right hand over her breast where he started rolling her nipple. He watched her eyes, and when she arched a little, when that wicked thing he did with his fingers seemed to send a hot shock of stimulation down to where he'd breached her, when she cried out with it—he started pumping.

"Yes. Yes." She curled her fingers into his hair and

clenched. She put her other hand on his shoulder, grasping and, eventually, clawing.

He stroked into her. Gentle movements initially, tender and tentative. During that time he still watched her, even as his movements became stronger. Hard, fast thrusts that huffed the breath out of her lungs.

She clutched at him and arched to meet him and murmured his name—then panted it, then screeched it. Finally, he gave over to it, not watching her but fully entering into it. Tensing and curling himself around her, caging her in like he was owning her, claiming her. Thrusting and then pounding into her, driven by her own exclamations of need, joining her with harsh, feral declarations of what he was doing to her, of what he wanted.

He'd taken to his knees in order to power his mighty thrusts into her. He maneuvered her legs so she was wrapped around him, unanchored, completely subject to his control.

He flexed and thrust and her body answered, a primal response known instinctively. She arched and shuddered, accepting him, giving herself up to his control.

It was primitive, like the mindless need to mate of ancestors eons past.

It was overwhelming, powerful, and incredibly exciting.

She came. She knew she had. It was a sweet, hot orgasm that had her shuddering and crying out. Nearly had her sinking down to the bed in repletion.

But Canaan seemed not to have noticed. He growled and kept pumping into her, squeezing her nipple harder now, using his teeth at the crook of her neck. Digging in with his knees, lifting her up off the bed so he could whale into her harder, deeper.

She'd thought she'd come, thought she'd had an orgasm. But that had been nothing. He thrust so deeply into her now, filling and stretching, an exquisite distention that stimulated sexual nerves she'd never suspected she had.

And suddenly, she was afraid. Suddenly, this little game she'd chosen to seduce him had turned on her. She wasn't snaring him so much as she was his, flagrantly owned and under his power.

His dark eyes suddenly opened, staring into hers. He grunted words, harsh directives and claims. "Come. Now.

Now, dammit. I've got you. You're fucking mine. Aren't you? *Come*. Scream with it."

It was all true, and she did exactly as he bade. Her body shuddered, spasming, wracking, wallowing in the power of his harsh penetrations, tossed on the sea of his devastating command.

She cried and rocked, opening herself to those final, unbearably rending thrusts. Her body seized, clutching to every part of him, giving the last strands of her hold on herself over to him.

But she wasn't alone in it. As she cried and bucked and screamed, she knew he was there with her, his own body buffeted by powerful quakes, his arms clutching around her, and his breath coming in harsh, howling groans and grunts.

She felt his release, deep inside her. Even with the condom, she felt the blast of that heat through her body, felt the shuddery surrender as he gave over his essence.

He was clutched around her, his breath still growling in her ear, harsh pants that matched her own.

He dropped his head onto her shoulder as they slowly settled. With his lips, he soothed where he'd bitten earlier.

She wasn't sure she could see. She wondered if she'd been struck blind. "That was good. So good. *Amazing*."

His palm took hold alongside her head and he turned her to face him. He nudged a little until she opened her eyes.

Oh. She *could* see. His beautiful face was there in front of hers, his dark eyes seeking hers.

She loved him. She'd thought it before, when she'd watched him play with Tino, when he'd leaned his cheek down to receive a kiss from Joss or Marta. When he'd stood with her in his arms and so carefully carried her to her car.

Now she knew it. Her heart sang with it, certain. She put a palm softly on his cheek and started to speak the words.

But his gaze hardened and he covered her mouth with his fingers. "Go to sleep, baby."

He held his fingers there until he could see her relent. Then he nudged her into rolling over, spooning her backside into his warmth. He pulled the light covers over them and settled so he breathed into her hair.

"Sleep, baby."

$\mathcal{C}$HAPTER FOUR

Josefina slept like she was in heaven, like she couldn't recall ever sleeping before. For as far back as she could recall, there had been no safety in sleep. It wasn't until she'd moved into the Hayes home that she was in a place where she could fall asleep at night and expect to lie undisturbed until morning.

But this was more. Canaan's strong arms wrapped around her, his solid body warm and steady behind her, gave her a sense of safe haven. Like he'd built a shelter of security around her, a place of trust. It was eminently dependable; she was utterly protected.

She woke alone.

Well, that was the third time she woke.

Once, she woke when Canaan had gotten up to make a trip to the bathroom. When he came back, he sat on the side of the bed and started the process of removing his prosthesis. She knew she was violating his privacy, but she rolled over to sit beside him and turned on the bedside light.

He looked at her stonily, but she met his gaze calmly for long enough that he let out a disgruntled sigh and proceeded. He popped the little mechanism that secured the prosthetic limb onto the sleeve that covered his leg from above the knee and down. He set it aside, then started peeling back the sleeve. It was close fitting and airtight, a strong enough seal to hold the prosthetic in place. Strong enough that, theoretically, a person could hang upside down by his or her prosthesis and it would still hold.

She imagined Canaan had tested that theory.

Inside the liner, he'd covered his residual limb with a sort of stocking. As he rolled it down, she put her hand on his thigh. It was all hard muscle that tightened with her touch.

The trauma that had cost him his lower leg had injured

his thigh as well. She traced the groove of a long scar that ran from mid-thigh to his knee and partially down the residual limb. Past his knee, instead of the thick tibial and calf muscles like on his right leg, there was a smooth stump that extended about halfway to where the ankle should be. It was thinner than his other lower leg, the muscle there having wasted some from lack of use.

It was striking, in light of Canaan's general strength and extremely competent physicality. But also, it seemed...simply a part of him.

She ran her hand over it, and he turned his face away.

"You don't have to hide it. It's nothing to be ashamed of."

"I know. I don't hide it. Not really."

"You never wear shorts."

"I do. I haven't, though, when I knew you and Tino were coming over."

"Why? I don't care. And Tino won't freak out or anything."

He finally turned his head back, and took her hand under his. "No, I don't suppose he will. But he surely will have questions."

She smiled. "No doubt."

He lifted her hand and kissed it, then moved aside so she could lie down again. "Go back to sleep. I didn't mean to wake you."

He lay down next to her and she tucked her head into his shoulder. Not given much choice, he wrapped his arm around her.

Seffie kissed his chest, reveling in the scent of him, the smooth skin over hard muscle. When her hand moved to slide down the hard slab of his abs, he grabbed it and secured it with his own. He touched his lips to her forehead. "Sleep," he said.

It happened once more, during the night, that she woke with Canaan curled behind her. His arm was wrapped around her waist and his erection pressed into her bottom. She arched a little, making more contact. Like he'd been awake, waiting, he squeezed his arm around her. Then he nudged back, separating so she no longer felt him pressing into her. Once more, he told her to sleep.

It was dawn the next time she woke, and he was gone.

She rolled over to face his side of the bed and, running her hand along his cool pillow and the mattress, knew that he'd been gone for a while. Her fingers bumped into a piece a paper, a small note with a single word—*milking.*

Looking around the room, she was aware of how little of himself he'd put there. Simple furnishings, clean surfaces. Against the wall, a thing she hadn't seen before, was a locked, heavily constructed metal cabinet, as tall as the door and twice as wide. A gun safe, she realized.

She waited until long past when the sun came up, sure that he would be back. It took her an embarrassingly long time to realize that he wasn't going to return. That, despite the interest his body had shown during the night, despite the way he'd sweetly held her, his urging her back to sleep and his absence in the morning were meant to send a clear signal.

He didn't want her again.

Making love to him had been spectacular. Admittedly, Josefina had essentially no experience to judge by, but still she was certain of that. It had been powerful and moving and...*spectacular*. She would have sworn it was the same for him. She couldn't fathom otherwise. Wouldn't.

Moving slowly, contemplating her circumstance, she used his shower. Then she used his toothbrush. If he objected, he should have stuck around to say so.

She found him in the barn, mucking out old, soiled hay and laying new. He worked steadily, the pitchfork like an extension of his own lithe muscles. He didn't stop, even when she was certain he knew she was there.

Finally, she stepped close enough to the hay bale he was working from that he had to pause or risk injuring her.

He thrust the fork down, piercing the ground very near her sandaled toes, and raised his gaze to hers. "Yeah?"

"Canaan."

"We did what you wanted. Aren't we done?"

So. He could be a bear when he felt like it.

"I didn't mean for us to be 'done.'"

"No? When do you see your pal, Trevor?"

"Canaan."

"When?" He was gruff, angry.

Seffie swallowed, uncertain now about the wisdom of this scheme she'd started. But he really didn't seem in the mood to hear it had all been a ploy. "He's been away this semester break week. He'll be back tomorrow."

"Well, have a good time with him."

"Canaan!" She reached out to touch his arm, but he backed away, looking dangerous even without the pitchfork in his hands.

"I gave you what you wanted, Sef. I'd appreciate it if you left me alone now."

Josefina was restless on Sunday. She should be studying, prepping for the summer semester that began on Monday. She'd taken a bit of a risk, spending so much of her week off at the farm rather than hitting the books. But the break had been good for her, she thought, and, at least for most of the week, she'd been happy with the progress she'd made with Canaan.

Though Saturday morning had been a major exception to that.

She'd done her best to put it out of her mind for the rest of Saturday and did, in fact, get a lot of work done for her histopath class.

But on Sunday, her mind had wandered. She'd tried to study, then took a break for a run. Then tried again, and interrupted herself to get her laundry done.

The next time she gave up, she biked to campus and sat outdoors on the quad with a cup of coffee and a textbook. Students were returning from their break activities, and she nodded and smiled at several of them. But she remained alone until someone set his own cup of coffee on the table and loomed over her, even once he'd sat across from her.

She looked up, startled. "Will."

"Josefina."

He took a sip of coffee and looked like he was going to be there for a while. He watched her carefully, and she had to make an effort to not fidget. "I'd think you'd be spending time with Trevor now that your break's ending."

Suppressing a swallow, she grasped for an explanation. "He—"

She stopped as he lifted a brow.

"Are you going to lie to me, Sef?" *Me*, he meant. *The sheriff's deputy*.

Josefina sighed and closed her book. "There is no Trevor. Well, there is, but he's just a friend."

"So why does Canaan think he's your boyfriend?"

"Canaan asked you to check up on me?"

"He asked me to make sure the guy you were hooked up with wasn't a skank."

She sighed again, heavier this time, louder. Kind of a moan.

"He cares about you. He wanted to make sure you wouldn't get hurt." He took a sip of coffee while Seffie looked away from his steady, resolute gaze. "Now I have to think about whether *he's* going to get hurt."

"I'm not going to hurt Canaan."

"You're lying to him."

"I love him." Seffie's voice shook a bit, so she paused. But she held Will's stern gaze while she took a sip of coffee. She set down her cup and cleared her throat. "Do you understand that Canaan doesn't think he's worthy of love? Or barely so anyway? That he thinks I'm a kid? That he believes he's been through more in his life than I could ever comprehend? Or *forgive*, if I knew?"

Will was a big guy, intimidating to Seffie for that reason alone. She'd seen him mainly in the context of two weddings, one of which was his own. In those settings, he'd seemed mellow and indulgent. He'd appeared sweetly and somewhat nervously enamored when he first met Katherine, and then utterly in love when he made her his wife.

But he was a big guy *and* a deputy, so when he sat across a table asking questions, it was reasonable to shake.

Seffie felt significant relief when, after a long moment, he sighed, ruffled one hand through his hair, and sat back in his chair. "I do understand those things. And I'm impressed and pleased that you do, too. But I pretty much go with the principle that you shouldn't lie to someone you love."

Seffie sat back, too. "It's a good principle."

"And so your purpose with the whole pretend Trevor thing was...?"

Seffie's cheeks warmed and she looked down at the table. "I wanted Canaan to make love to me. I...I thought he was attracted to me, but he was avoiding me—not speaking to me beyond whatever greeting was required, not even making eye contact." She sighed again. "I told him I had a boyfriend. I asked him to make love to me because I was afraid." She lifted her head and met Will's gaze. "Bad things happened to me when I was young."

Seffie waited for Will to nod his acknowledgment before she went on.

"I told Canaan I wanted my first time to be with someone I trusted. That part was true. All of it was, except for the bit about the boyfriend."

Will folded his arms across his chest and looked off over the quad. He took a deep breath and then a couple more. He didn't look at her right away when he spoke. "You have to tell him, Sef." He turned his head then to make eye contact. "You have to, or I will." He waved away her objection and went on. "You and I are connected, Josefina. Leet and Sadie are my friends and Tino is theirs. He's yours, too. That puts you under the umbrella of people I care about. That means I will always do what I can to help you."

Seffie knew what he said was true, and that it was no small thing. She'd heard Katherine speak of it—Will's firm resolve, the basic character of his nature that had him taking care of the entire world around him. It applied to those he loved whether they wanted it or not.

"But my first loyalty in this instance is to Canaan. It wouldn't be right for me to know this thing and not tell him. Do you understand?"

Seffie nodded. "Yes." It was a man's code, not a thing that brooked argument.

He returned her nod. "I can give you a week."

Then he stood and left.

Josefina had class all day Monday, but she skipped her study group to go to the farm. She'd delayed until nearly dark, until she could be reasonably certain that Canaan would be in his home.

She'd called it right. Before she stepped up onto the porch, she could see him in the living room. He was stretched out on his deep leather sofa, a book held open on his chest, a reading lamp above his head the only illumination inside the house.

She was pretty sure he'd heard her car when she drove up to the A-frame. And certain he'd recognized her footsteps when she walked up to the door. But his only response when she knocked was to douse his reading lamp. She didn't understand why he wanted it dark before he opened the door to her.

Until she understood that he didn't intend to open the door to her at all. Until she realized that small sound she'd heard was the snick of the lock.

After long minutes passed, she dropped her forehead onto the hard wood, barely keeping from knocking her head against it. "Canaan." She didn't speak loudly. She knew he would be close, would hear. "I have to talk to you. I'm not leaving until I do."

Apparently, he was unmoved.

She let more minutes pass until she lifted her head. She pressed her palms against the door, imagining she could feel his heat there, just beyond. "I'll be over here, in the glider, when you're ready."

The glider was at the west end of the porch, facing out toward the yard and the sunset. She watched the light fall from the sky, gently rocking with a toe that barely reached the deck. When it was full dark and she was still alone, she curled over onto her side.

It was past dawn when she woke, wrapped with a woven cotton blanket in a Native American design. She knew the milking would be done, and the old farm truck was gone from beside the barn.

He'd left her on the porch all night and then escaped.

Josefina stood up and stretched out the kinks. She folded the blanket and left it at his door.

Maybe some women would be discouraged. But she smiled as she went to her car. She had him on the run.

Canaan cursed when Josefina drove into the yard again on Wednesday evening. He was in the barn after completing a workout, had picked up his guitar, and was wallowing in the misery of goats for company.

He clearly couldn't leave the girl on his porch overnight again. Joss knew everything that happened on the farm. She might not have commented, but she'd obviously blabbed to Marta, who of course couldn't hold back from shaming him about it.

And he should be ashamed. First he'd refused to answer her knock and even locked her out. He guessed that was the first time his door had been locked since he'd moved into the A-frame. Then he'd left her sleeping in his glider—and sneaking out to cover her with a blanket hardly earned him any points.

So he figured he ought to man up and face her, though he surely didn't want to.

Making love to her had about killed him. Well, making love to her had been freaking heaven. Holding back from taking her again—and again—had about killed him.

Wanting her, knowing he shouldn't and couldn't have her, well...*that* was hell.

He'd spent about every moment of every day since Saturday wishing it could be different. It was true he wasn't as crazy as he used to be. He could be trusted to stay sane most of the time.

Joss thought so. He'd been very aware that she'd never left him alone with the animals when he'd first come to the farm. She'd never spoken about it, but it had taken a few weeks to gain her trust. Then Sadie and the kids had come, and Joss had watched him again. Joss was subtle about it— probably even Sadie had never noticed. But it was a couple more months before he was trusted to be alone with any of them, and a lot of months before Tino was allowed to come out to the yard or the barn alone.

He could trust that if Joss thought Sef wasn't safe in his hands, she'd have told him one way or another.

Maybe her standards were lower than his. All he knew was he wasn't taking chances with Seffie.

He still woke up some nights with the terrors. Not so often any more, but not never either. Even within the month, he'd woken in a panic, started reaching for his weapons and gear, and tried tearing out for shelter before he remembered he was safe in his house. Or that he was missing one foot. He'd ended up plastered flat on his bedroom floor before it all came back to him.

That was the reason he hadn't slept all Friday night. He'd held Sef in his arms, held her and *yearned* for her, but he hadn't slept. He couldn't spend his life sleeping with a woman and not *sleeping*.

He'd hit the booze and the drugs pretty hard until he'd reached bottom up there in Montreal. He'd done okay staying off it since he'd come to the farm. Except for the night he'd tied one on celebrating in Nashville, those wedding occasions when Seffie had noticed his two-drink limit had been about the only times he'd drunk since he'd dried out. He'd done that in all its unattractive splendor, hiding out in the barn back during those first days on the farm.

But it still called to him. And he hadn't resisted the call for long enough that he was sure he was done with it.

He was too big a risk. And Sef was too young, too inno-cent—despite her history—and had too much potential to be burdened with him. She was going to be a doctor, for God's sake. She'd probably end up heir to the cardiology empire that Leet's parents had built.

Last thing she needed was a handicapped, ex-drunk, barely sane goat herder holding her back.

But as he watched from the barn like a coward, she walked up onto his porch and sat in one of his chairs. Like she didn't have the sense God gave the damn goats.

Sef wasn't stupid, so when Canaan walked—stalked—out of the barn soon after she'd sat down, she got up and went to stand right in front of his door. He came and stood before her, close, and going out of his way to look intimidating.

"I suppose you think we have to talk."

"Not really." Not yet anyway. She still had most of a week. On Monday, she'd meant to tell him of her deception. She'd felt the burden of it, the weight of Will's calm eyes im-pressing upon her that she was doing the wrong thing. That she had to be better.

But then Canaan had left her sleeping on his front porch

all night, and she was no longer feeling so sympathetic toward him. It could wait.

His eyes flared, and he searched hers for a long moment.
She didn't back down from the challenge. She could see the
muscles flex that kept his jaw clenched. After a good bit of
that, he reached his hand out to open the door behind her
back.

It just happened that his wrist and forearm slid along her
waist while he did it. And when it was done, he ended with
his hand gripping into her skirt.

She'd worn a short little cotton swing skirt for class, with
a tightly fitting halter-top that ended a couple inches above
the waist. Except for her wedged sandals, the only other
thing she wore was a white satin thong.

Somehow, that was a thing he seemed to know. As he
bunched the fabric of her skirt up in his fist at her hip, he
managed to capture the band of her thong in it, too. He
turned his hand, rolling it a bit, and drew the thong up tight-
er into her center.

Her lips parted and her breath came in a quiet gasp. He
was aware of that, too, his gaze hot on her mouth. His
mouth close to hers.

With his hand on her hip, he pushed her two steps into
the house, just enough that he could close the door behind
them. Then he turned her and hauled her up against the
door.

His whole body was hard against her. His muscled thighs
pressed into hers. His rigid chest compressed her breasts
and held her back firmly to the door. His mouth took hers,
fully, deeply.

With his right hand, Canaan rucked her skirt up until he
reached bare skin. He twisted that satin band in his fingers
again, tugging it back and forward so the thong sawed into
her a little, both front and back. Josefina moaned, feeling the
hot wetness of her own excitement as he tormented her.

He pushed his left hand between their chests and tugged
at the buttons that closed her top. He went only far enough
to bare one breast then he palmed her roughly, chafing his
hand over her hard nipple.

He left her mouth to drag his tongue along her neck.
Then he nipped and sucked, and Seffie was certain he left a

deliberate mark.

"I can smell you." It was a growl, a hot, satisfied pro-nouncement. "You're fucking wet."

Yes.

He let go with both his hands for a moment, keeping her propped against the door with his body. They were pressed so close that it was no mystery what his hands were doing.

When he came back to her, he lifted her by the hips, hooking his forearms under her thighs to wrap them around his waist. He reached between them, tugging the thong aside and pressed hotly against her opening.

He sank his face into the crook of her shoulder and curs-ed. "I don't have a condom on."

Seffie lifted her arms to his shoulders, grasping the hair at the back of his head with one hand. "It doesn't matter. I have an IUD."

"But you're fucking two men."

"No, I'm not."

He lifted his head to look at her, trying to see something in her eyes. "You know what? I don't fucking care."

He shoved into her then, all the way, and she moaned, *moaned*. It felt so very good, so exquisitely *right* to be filled with him, to have that solid, tangible connection. She gripped him, one hand in his hair and the other hooked around his shoulder.

His own groan rumbled through his chest. She arched, preparing for the hard taking she thought was coming. But he held there, his head buried into the crook of her neck now. He turned enough that his lips were at her ear. "Are you okay? Sef?"

"Don't stop. Canaan." She was aware of his control, awed by the exquisite torture it was that he paused, checked him-self. She could feel the trembling leash he held on the pow-erful urges that drove him.

It was so unnecessary. She wanted all that he could give her, wanted him to thrust into her, to take her, to *have* her. "Canaan. Cane."

He growled darkly and circled his arms around her, one at her hips and one behind her back. He squeezed hard, stir-ring her breasts with the solid mass of his chest. Then he flexed, pressing deeply into her and holding there for several harsh breaths.

"Oh. Oh." Seffie rolled her head back against the door, lost to the power of it—the scent of him that filled her head, the incredible hard strength in the way he held her, pene-trated her.

He started moving then, like a machine, steady, deter-mined, driven thrusts. Her breaths and his matched, moans and groans, satisfied and needy at the same time. They clutched hard against each other, rising together until they both cried out, both spasmed into harsh orgasms.

Seffie felt that liquid heat as he gave over to her, a hot, fulfilling exchange. She savored it, relished the fact he leaned hard into her, hard into the door, as though he were nearly felled. That he seemed to have as much trouble finding his breath as she did.

It was a long time before he lifted her off of him. He set her on her feet, steadying them both with hands firm on her hips. She reached up to touch his face, but he intercepted her hand and held it away from him. The soft, satiated look in his eyes hardened.

Without a word, he nudged her a couple steps to the side, opened the door, nudged her again until she was across the threshold. Then he stepped back and closed the door in her face.

Sef came again Thursday evening.

Canaan was feeling like a jerk for having taken her against the door like that and then putting her out like a nui-sance cat. He was uncomfortable to even face the moms and so he'd stayed scarce the whole day, rudely not even letting them know he wouldn't be in for meals.

He hid out in the barn, pretending he didn't hear Sef's car drive up at end evening twilight. But she found him anyway, with that damn Canaan Liberty radar she appeared to have. She'd gone to the A-frame first, but her super Spidey-senses apparently let her know in about a second that he wasn't there.

Like she knew right where he was, she walked up to him in the dark of the barn. He was resting back in a pile of hay, and did nothing more than set his guitar aside before she climbed onto him.

They made love there in the hay. More like love this time, with her kissing him in a way he couldn't resist, soft touches and softer words. He took her gently this time, like a man ought to do with the woman he loved.

It scared the bejesus out of him.

She'd fallen asleep on top of him, after he'd made her come three times and he'd finally poured himself into her.

They spent the night there, Canaan awake for the whole length of it so he didn't wake up all fight-or-flight with her defenseless in his arms. He was perfectly happy, too—perfectly, *blissfully* happy—doing nothing more than lying there with her.

Which was the main cause of the whole bejesus thing.

He ducked out from under her at milking time. She found him an hour later. She was still sweetly mussed from a night spent making love then sleeping in a barn, and, on top of that, gorgeously lit up by pure dawn light. She caught him nudged in between a couple of does and put her mouth on his.

She'd already gotten him started thinking the damn goats could wait when she pulled back, turned, and walked away. He didn't stop watching the sway of her ass until she was out of sight, despite the impatient bleat of the milker he left unattended.

He manned up a bit and went into the farmhouse for breakfast. Marta gave him a kiss and a smile, but Joss opened her mouth with what he knew would be the set-down he deserved.

He stopped her with a raised hand. "Can we *please* not talk about it?"

The two women did that little exchange of looks thing that often sufficed for communication between them, and Joss relented. He must have looked fucking pitiful.

They had a nearly silent meal and, when it was over, Canaan asked Joss if she'd take care of the next morning milking. When she agreed, he told them he'd try to be back for the chore on Saturday evening.

Then he went to his place and outfitted his pack. He loaded it with a tarp, his blanket roll, jerky, trail mix, a couple pieces of fruit, and water.

His favorite way up Mount Washington was from the east. He liked to take the Tuckerman Ravine trail up to the summit and then circle back down on Lion Head. Last summer, he'd made it at a run as far as Hermit Lake. This year, his plan was to get to the Headwall before he had to slow to a walk. There weren't many guys even with two legs who could take that steep, narrow trail at a run.

Though he could have, and his buddies with him, back in his days spent in the Hindu Kush. With full pack.

His circumstances had changed, and his abilities with them. At least the first part of that was good.

Either way, that was what he wanted. Nothing but rock and silence. His skill and determination against nature's indifference. No mothers to frown and make him feel guilty. No little hottie who wanted him to love her, but not *love* her.

Not even any goats. Not even of the mountain sort.

*C*HAPTER FIVE

"You gotta milk? That's your excuse?" Will lobbed his stinky wet towel at him.

Luckily, the man's throwing arm had been worn down by the trouncing the skins had just dealt to the shirts, and the towel hit the bench with a wet splat.

They'd greeted each other first thing outside the gym when Will drove up in his truck. Canaan had looked at him in question, and Will had held his gaze for a bit. Then he looked off to the horizon. "He's not a skank." Canaan waited long enough to know that was all Will was going to say, then walked away in disgust. He figured it was the unsaid stuff that was going to kill him.

He'd come down off the mountain in time to make Saturday morning basketball. He'd been right to go up—he'd run until his muscles burned, until his lungs were sawing for air, and then he'd slept solid, with only a couple blankets and a tarp sheltering him from both earth and sky. He'd got up with the sun and loped down the trail back to his truck.

He felt better. Or, at least he had, until the unsaid shit and two hours of hard ball had him collapsing on the bleachers.

Leet Hayes and his son Jace were there, and Will, and some other dudes from town. Canaan had played in the league for a couple years now and knew most of the guys pretty well. Well enough that when he stripped down to his shorts, nobody freaked, and nobody held back on the court. Anymore.

Canaan had just turned down Leet's invitation to a barbeque later in the day. And, yeah, he'd used a lame pretext for it. But he was pretty sure that if he was being invited, so was a certain young hottie.

"Who's going to be there?"

"What are we, girls? What the hell does it matter who's

going to be there?" Will apparently didn't respect that ploy any better. "The man has steaks and good beer. Sadie makes the best potato salad in the state. And the moms are bringing pie."

"Is Kate making eggs?"

That earned him a wet shirt that would have slapped him in the face but for his lightning-quick reflexes. He tossed it back in objection. Everybody knew Kate couldn't cook.

Other than eggs, or so said Will.

Leet was more decent about it and answered him evenly. "Just us. Sadie and the kids. The moms. Ray and Lourdes and their baby. Will and Kate and the sprout. My parents."

Of course, Will couldn't keep a sock in it. "He wants to know if Sef is going to be there."

"Sef? Yeah?" Leet looked over, and Canaan had a devil of a time putting up a steady gaze. "Uh, yeah. I think so. She's invited anyway."

Canaan wouldn't say he dawdled over the evening milking, but he didn't hurry it along either. By the time he got to Leet's, everybody was sitting down to dinner.

Leet had a great place, a home and studio he'd had built out of glass and wood and stone. He pretty much owned the hill it was on—a creek along the side of the property, and a nice pond out back with plenty of hillside beyond that.

He was a pro football player turning metal sculptor. He built these fantastic trees with intricate branches that ended in thousands of dangling leaves. Like natural trees, they moved with the breeze, kinetic and musical. Beautiful. And wild, in a storm.

There were clusters of finished pieces, like a forest, on the terrace outside his studio, and more of them scattered along the pond and hillside. It made a spectacular, fantastical setting.

It appeared the pond had gotten some use. Jace and Tino were still in wet swim trunks, and Sef was in a bikini top and some sort of all-but-transparent wrap slung low beneath her waist.

He considered asking Will to arrest her, but he wasn't entirely sure about the state laws with regard to indecent exposure.

Apparently, once the grilling was done, the babies had been passed to the men so the women could all gather together in their little gaggle. One of the toddlers, Rachel, sat on her grandpa's lap, thinking nothing of plastering her wet swimsuit against the chairman of cardiology. The other belonged to Ray, Leet's old high school coach and one time father-in-law, and Ray had that little tyke hiked up on his hip. Sadie and Leet's second baby and Will and Kate's first were too close in age for him to tell them apart, but he figured it was a safe guess that the one sacked out against Leet's shoulder was his, and the one Will seemed to be burping belonged to him.

It should have been awkward, stepping up to that tableau of loving families and close friends, but it wasn't. Every last one of them greeted him—anything from a friendly nod to Tino's flying leap and wet hug. The women all required a kiss as he rounded that table, a thing that felt entirely comfortable from every one of them except Leet's mom—the prior cardiology chairwoman—and the hottie in the bikini. In the first case, it was just that he didn't know Aletha Hayes all that well and, truth be told, she was a little scary.

In the second, it was that he didn't want to straighten up from the kiss sporting a wicked, conspicuous boner. And he didn't know how to kiss her—all warm, tanned skin and hot, nearly naked curves—without that being a problem.

He took so much caution about it, in fact, that his lips totally missed hers.

Though he didn't miss the haughty way she lifted her brow about it.

In strategic retreat, he loaded up a plate and sought the safety of the man/baby table. He set his dinner down in a spot between Will and Jace. Before he sat, he saw Tino was struggling with his steak, so he walked over, stood behind him, and cut it into bite-sized pieces. Next to Tino, Leet watched what he was doing.

When the job was done, Leet looked at his own steak and then handed his baby up. "Do you mind?"

The ranch in Kansas where Canaan had grown up was ever filled with kids and babies. It was a family spread, expanded over a century and a half, with aunts and uncles and cousins working it, and those folks were all big reproducers. So it wasn't strange to him to be handed a baby, and Canaan tucked the sleeping bundle—a boy named Grayson, he'd learned—up against his shoulder without thought.

The abrupt quiet, however, reminded him that he wasn't in Kansas anymore. Surprised into feeling guilty, he looked up and saw that nearly the whole table of women had stopped what they were doing to look at him.

He froze, suddenly nervous, until Joss turned. She had her back to him and was in the middle of a story when she realized she'd lost her audience. She swiveled her head around to see what was so interesting, and gave him a good once-over. Then, like it was nothing, she turned back to the table and her story.

Meanwhile, Will, eyes on the women's table, breathed out a gentle curse. "Jesus. Look at them. They all think that's hot. We're all going to get lucky tonight. Tino, you close your ears, and, Jace, I'm not talking about you. Here, Cane, come take this one, too."

Will held his daughter in the air like a sacrifice to the gods. Canaan chuckled and let Leet finish cutting his steak before he traded one baby for the other. This one was awake, so he sat and plopped her little butt down next to his plate, propping her with his big hands so she could look up at him. When he nuzzled her, she curled her fingers into a strand of his hair and gazed up with big green eyes like she owned his soul, just as she fully expected to.

Without moving his head, he glanced over at her beauty of a mother. "Hell. You're sunk, dude, aren't you?"

Will nodded glumly. "Yeah." He poked a finger at a little chubby flesh, the baby equivalent of a punch to the arm. "But we've already made an agreement, haven't we, Vivvie? She gets to have all the sex she wants." He looked hard into Canaan's eyes, serious as shit. "After I'm dead."

Two elbows and at least three kicks to her shin under the table made sure that Josefina noticed the way Canaan so naturally handled those babies. She'd been watching even before that, when he'd casually, spontaneously leaned over Tino to cut his steak.

Like she needed help figuring out that Canaan was exactly the man she wanted. *No*, she didn't need help with that.

What she needed help with was facing Will's intent, questioning eyes.

She'd done what she could to avoid him through the early part of the party. She'd played in the pond with Jace and Tino, then helped in the kitchen while Will joined the man-group at the grill.

After they'd eaten, it was mostly women doing cleanup, as the majority of the guys had kids sacked out on them—an excuse they good-naturedly made the most of. Canaan was baby-less and so he stood and helped out, but he was avoiding her with about the same determination that she was avoiding Will.

Once the work was done, when it was determined that they should climb the hill beyond the pond for the best view of the sunset, her luck ran out. There was a gentle trail through the woods, wide enough for two to walk alongside each other. And about halfway up, it was Will walking alongside her.

"It's been a week, Josefina. You haven't told him yet, have you?"

"It's a week tomorrow, Will. I'll tell him."

He wasn't happy. "You know you have to."

She sighed, aware she didn't have a right to anger. "I know. I meant to on Monday. But—"

"But he left you out on the porch all night."

She raised a brow, and he shrugged. "Joss talks. Marta talks. Sadie talks. Katherine talks. It's how I know about half of what goes on in my town."

Seffie stayed silent.

"Well, he can be a stinker, no doubt. But still, you have to tell him. I've invited him over to my place for a beer tomorrow evening. If he doesn't know by then, he's hearing it from me."

Canaan had seen that conversation and knew that shit

was coming. Will had spent the evening on low alert. Canaan could feel the man's eyes on him whenever Sef came in proximity, or whenever he was watching her. Which was most of the time.

And a lot of the rest of the time, Will was watching Sef. Then he'd not so casually cut her out of the herd when they were walking up Hayes Mountain, as Leet liked to call it.

Neither Will nor Sef was happy with what was said between them.

They weren't talking about the weather. He didn't imagine the two of them had anything serious to discuss besides him.

In this particular case, he didn't see any advantage to hanging around to hear bad news. He avoided both them and the issue by tagging onto a cluster of the women as they headed back down the hill after a spectacular sunset. Kate was carrying the sprout, and Canaan knew she bit her tongue when he took the sleeping baby from her for the return hike. He could see the wheels of her bright mind spin and knew she guessed correctly that he'd be offended if she showed any doubt about his ability to carry the baby safely.

He rolled his eyes when she turned to look behind her, having absolutely no doubt she was looking for a nod from her damned husband. She must have gotten it, because she paid no further attention to him and her child, but got all into girl-midwife-baby shit with Sadie.

When they got back to the house, Will silently took Vivienne from him. It didn't take words.

With a nod and a heavy sigh, Canaan sought diversionary tactics. There was no reason to invite whatever heartbreak was coming. So he grabbed Tino, tossed him up over his shoulder, and lugged him up the stairs to the upper deck. He set the kid on his feet there, patted his butt, and shamelessly lied.

"Sef said she was going to read your bedtime story tonight. I think she's in the kitchen."

They said goodnight and the boy headed off. Canaan went back down to say goodbye to the rest of the crowd. On the way home, alone in his truck, he let out the curses he'd been holding back.

The trouble with having a friend, and then asking him for

help, was that he ended up knowing all your shit. Shit you might not want to know yourself.

At his home, he moved around in the dark. He lit a couple candles in the bedroom and turned down the sheet and light blanket. He'd unloaded the trash and the water bottle from his pack, but the tarp and bedroll were still there. He refilled the water bottle and set the pack behind the door.

He knew she'd come. He'd have her once more, sure it would be the last time. But he didn't have to stay around for the rest of it.

He'd camouflaged himself in the Hindu Kush, silent and invisible while Al-Qaeda soldiers trooped past him not ten feet away. Surely there was someplace on this damn farm he could hide that she couldn't find.

Josefina wasn't an idiot, so she wasn't surprised that Canaan was gone when she came out of Tino's room. She'd recognized the tactic for what it was, but certainly wasn't going to let Tino down while two supposed adults worked out their squabble.

It wasn't like she didn't know where the stubborn, childish, shameless man lived.

She delayed a little, taking a last glass of wine with Sadie and Leet on the deck as the moon rose. The three of them were nearly completely comfortable with each other now, having circled long enough around the issues related to their unique bond to one little boy. She knew that Leet especially had been fearful that she would change her mind about the adoption. She'd tried hard to let him know that Tino was safely in their hands, at the same time she meant to make clear it wasn't Leet's very big and slightly scary presence that had made it happen.

That had been all Sadie. From the beginning, her open heart had let Seffie call the shots, assuring her that she could give Sadie as much of Tino as she wanted and no more. Sadie hadn't talked about adoption until they were both certain Sef was ready for it, and Sef was pretty sure Sadie would have stood up to her giant of a husband if Sef hadn't agreed.

It was complicated. But they were working through it, and they were succeeding at the one thing they all wanted—raising a happy, healthy boy. And now, she was having to explain to Leet what a *bō* staff was and why his son was running around whacking everything with a stick. He went on to take Sadie to task about her mother pushing baby goats on the family, and Sef was glad to be excused from that one.

She got hugs from both of them when she left—long and sweet from Sadie, shorter but still real from Leet. Their arms were around each other as they watched her leave, wishing her well.

Their mouths to God's ear.

Canaan's house was dark when she drove up. The yard was empty and the porch, too. But she didn't have to see him to know when he was present—she never had. When she opened the front door—unlocked, for a change—she knew he was inside. She took a couple more steps and saw the flicker of candlelight from his bedroom.

He stood on the far side of the bed, his back to the glass doors that let out onto the side deck. His eyes were waiting for hers, barely visible in the flutter of light. The bed was open.

"We have to talk."

"No," he said. "We don't."

She went a step further, into his room. "Canaan."

He pointed to the bed. "That's your option. Lie down there, or go."

Sef could tell which his preference was—or, at least, what his body wanted. He'd undressed and wore only a pair of pajama pants slung low on his hips. Nothing about the soft flannel hid the way he stirred beneath.

The candlelight caressed his body like a lover. Smooth skin over hard bulges of muscle, dark mysterious shadows, faint outlines of scars. The glimmering line of soft hair that arrowed down below his waist.

She would have this man. Perhaps it wouldn't be words that let him know.

Sef had changed clothes when she went upstairs in Leet's house at Tino's request for a story. She'd put on a short, tight knit skirt and a thin-strapped corset top that hooked up the front. She wore a thong underneath the skirt and a pair of sandals.

Now, she went no further to help him out than to kick off the sandals. Then she lay down on his bed.

When he came over her, he gave her almost all of his weight. He seemed to know exactly how much pressure from his muscled body felt precisely right. Enough to feel owned by him, taken. Not enough to feel overwhelmed or afraid.

He was on his elbows, securing her head in his hands, looking down at her. With exquisite tenderness, he leaned in to kiss her.

He made gentle, adoring love to her mouth. Soft brushes that left her lips tingling. Rough, drawing kisses that shot pleasure through her body, tightening her breasts and her loins.

Of their own accord, her hands rose. Her fingers stroked the smooth skin of his sides, the ripples of muscle and rib. He moaned and shuddered a little, the hard length of his erection burrowing into the valley between her thighs. She rocked her pelvis, welcoming him.

Lifting up, he stared down at her. Then, with one hand, he started unfastening her top. One hook at a time, he opened it until it fell to either side, leaving her totally exposed to him.

He looked at her, his breath harsh. The heat of his gaze caused her nipples to furl, calling for his attention. He went back to both elbows, letting himself down over her until his chest pressed against her nipples. He watched her again, moving his chest over her, stimulating her with the gentle abrasion of skin over sensitive skin.

She arched up on a moan, seeking more. But he lifted away, keeping control of the pleasure he gave her.

She closed her eyes, turning her head in frustration. "Canaan."

"Open your eyes. Look at me."

Mindlessly tractable, she did what he asked. What he bade.

"Don't stop looking at me."

He pressed harder, compressing her breasts, so his next movements caused a firm rasp against her nipples. His face was close over hers, their breath shared. His fingers tightened in her hair, securing her for—

For the hard thrust of his pelvis against hers. She cried out, feeling the solid length of him against her most sensitive place. He rubbed against her a little, drawing little shivers and moans from her.

His breath was hot and harsh; his eyes glittered fiercely. He swooped in to kiss her roughly once more then lifted up to capture her gaze again. Leaning to his left, he reached down to tug her skirt along her hips. When it was low enough, he found the black band of her thong and curled his fingers into it. He wrapped it around his hand to pull it tight against her, then stroked his thumb over her center, the silk there a useless barrier against his burning touch.

He liked her response to that. She could see it in the hot flare of his eyes. Deliberately, he pulled against her breasts and flicked his thumb over her.

Her breath shuddered in and out as he drove her up. She dug her heels into the bed, seeking more. But he held back, staying in control until she panted in frustration.

"Canaan!"

She said more, his name again and rough curses, until something of it satisfied him.

"Lift up."

He took that wicked thumb away from her and the pressure against her breasts, too. He shimmied her skirt and thong down until she could kick them away. He did the same with his flannels.

Then, without any pause or a bit of warning, he thrust into her. He was on top of her again, his weight confining her like before. Except that he had her filled now, his body not only containing hers but penetrating it as well.

Her breath caught and she stared up at him. He met her gaze in challenge, daring her to object.

He didn't give her long. He tightened the grasp he had in her hair, both hands securing her. And then he began to thrust, hard, filling, conquering lunges that took her completely each time. He paused at the peak of every thrust, watching her eyes, making plain his possession.

Sef was lost to it. He held her helpless, her legs snared by his, her head captured between his hands, her gaze locked with his. Her body breached by his. His claim staked.

He moved faster and faster, still driving deeply into her,

his muscled body flexing relentlessly, precise and determined.

He watched every bit of what he did to her. Watched her
quicken, her breath fast and desperate, her body tense and
shivering. Watched her breaths turn to moans, her shivers
turn to shudders and then spasms.

Once she tried to turn her head and close her eyes, but
he wrenched her back. He kept her clenched beneath him
until she wracked into orgasm, bucking and crying out. He
joined her then, pistoning roughly into her, letting loose a
feral howl as he went over with her, clutching at her, filling
her.

Finally, finally, he released her gaze and dropped his
head to the mattress beside her. He rolled a little, letting his
weight fall away so her desperate lungs could gasp for air.
His chest worked hard, too, drawing rough breaths.

It was several minutes before their breathing steadied.
When she found her balance, Sef turned her face to him
again. Without looking at her, he turned his face away so she
had to speak to the back of his head.

"I love you, Canaan. You're the man I want. I want you
to marry me. I want it to be my baby you hold on your
shoulder."

"She told you?"

"Told me what?"

Will stared hard at Canaan, and Canaan stared hard back.

He hadn't been too cowardly to duck out on Sef when
she'd handed over her heart Saturday night, but he was too
cowardly to not show when Will insisted he come by for a
beer on Sunday evening.

Kate had greeted Canaan at the door and then gone off
on the pretext of nursing the baby. Will's dog Beowulf had
become Vivienne's self-designated protector and had followed dutifully behind the womenfolk. Will had opened a
couple of IPAs, handed him one, and then led him upstairs to
the upper deck. It had two nice teak recliners and a great
view of the village, with hills and the river beyond. Canaan
knew Will liked to survey his kingdom from there.

Will sighed, clearly weighing his words and wondering how big of an idiot he'd buddied up with. "There's no boyfriend. No Trevor. Well, there is this guy Trevor in her group of pals. But they don't have anything going on. Though he mighta tried."

Canaan's jaw flexed, his teeth grinding down until it hurt. "No. She didn't tell me that." He didn't bother to add he'd forbidden her to speak last night. He looked enough an idiot as it was.

No Trevor. He supposed it didn't matter. Except for the fact that it made him a fucking moron not to have seen that coming.

And her a fucking liar.

"She just told me she loves me and wants to have my babies."

Will waited a minute, like he was very good at doing. "Is there something wrong with that?"

"Well, let's see. You're telling me she lied to get what she wanted. That's a thing. Plus, she's brilliant, and in a few years, she'll be queen of some part of the medical world, surrounded by equally brilliant people sucking up to her. And I'm a damn goat farmer."

"And a cripple."

"Shut the fuck up."

"So it's not about your peg leg." Will didn't have any trouble in the face of Canaan's threatening glare, and the easy acceptance in his eyes made it hard to keep up a good mad. "It's not about those things you mentioned either, though I can see why you wouldn't be happy she lied to you. I'm sure you can suss out why she did. So, what is it about?"

There wasn't an easy answer, not one to say out loud, anyway, so Canaan was silent. In the meantime, Kate came and stood at the open doors. She was a woman and a damn therapist to boot, so she was genetically engineered to nose in. He had to give her credit, though, since she stood there and waited until Canaan nodded his agreement. It couldn't get worse, could it?

She touched his shoulder as she passed then went to Will. He automatically scooted over a bit and lifted his arms until she was settled alongside him, like they spent all their deck time together nestled in the same chair. She had her chin resting on Will's chest and looked over at Canaan. She hadn't brought a baby monitor deal, so he figured Beowulf was standing guard at the sprout's crib.

Will brought her up to date. "Josefina wants to have his babies. I'm not sure I have all the details, but she lied about having a boyfriend, and somehow, that's worse than if she really did have a boyfriend."

"I didn't say it was worse," Canaan mumbled, not really expecting anyone to care.

Kate perused Canaan, but it was a pretty soft look. So he wasn't prepared for it when she lopped him upside the head with her words.

"It got her into his bed. He would have refused if she'd approached him directly. So she said she had a boyfriend, and she was afraid to be with him sexually because of her history of abuse. She wanted her first experiences to be with someone she could trust. Ergo, she asked Canaan. He's entirely honorable and trustworthy, and she knew he wouldn't turn down her request for help. It was a perfectly sensible plan."

Fucking *ergo*. Canaan didn't know what fucking pissed him off the most—that fact that he hadn't considered Sef's underlying motivation, or that she'd blabbed about the whole thing. "She told you that?"

Kate lifted an elegant, eloquent brow, and Will rolled his eyes. "*Dude.*"

The therapist met his gaze until he had to close his eyes and turn away. *Okay*, so she could figure out the dynamics with Will's two sentences, while Canaan hadn't had a clue even when he'd spent weeks living it. He sighed out a big breath before taking a long slug of beer.

He opened his eyes on another suffering sigh while the couple went on talking as though he wasn't there.

"So he's a little pissed about the lie, and making up this crap about how she's too smart for him."

"An obvious smokescreen."

"Yeah." Will paused. "For what?"

There was another silence before Kate spoke. "Canaan?"

It was a gentle nudge, and Canaan figured she already knew anyway. But this was no doubt one of those therapeutic moments, when the crazy one was supposed to identify the "issues" on his own.

"I've already had a lot of therapy for PTSD, Kate. The VA actually knows what it's doing there." Though it had taken them some damn time.

"You've gotten a lot better."

"Yes."

"But..."

He couldn't look at her. She obviously wouldn't judge, and Will wouldn't either. Still, staring off over the village—the couple of church steeples, the mountains beyond—was the best he could manage. "I still have nightmares. I still wake up in a panic sometimes, forgetting where I am. Even forgetting that I'm missing part of my leg."

She was quiet for a moment, those sharp gears in her head working. "You know that's normal. You're not afraid you're crazy." She said that like it was a simple thing. If she only knew. "You're afraid you'll hurt her."

It was more than that. Sure, he knew the stages of healing. He could understand he'd made a lot of progress, better by far than a lot of men had done. Even so, it was asking a lot, to trust someone enough to let her see you wake up terrified and unnerved. Unmanned.

A man couldn't do that and still expect to see love in a woman's eyes.

But, yeah. There were those seconds when he wouldn't know where he was, wouldn't remember that he was safe, on the farm. In those moments, he was ready to kill. He'd done what he could, locking all his weapons in a gun safe. The key to it was in a strong box in the barn, so there was no way he could get to a gun before he woke—*really* woke. He didn't keep even a knife near his bed. But he wouldn't need a knife or anything else besides his hands to hurt Seffie. Worse than hurt her.

Kate's sharp, intelligent gaze was still on him, still considering. He could feel it.

"You've never fallen asleep with her, have you? You stay awake, protecting her."

Finally, he looked over. As expected, Kate's gentle gaze was on him. And he saw Will lift his head to kiss her temple.

Canaan flexed his jaw again, suppressing a little inclination to cry like a baby.

These two had done it. They'd found bone-deep love and

trust that surmounted Will's history of phobia and panic attacks.

To an extent, their love had healed Will. He'd faced every nightmare fear to protect Katherine, to rescue her from a maniac.

Canaan envied them, wishing it could be the same for him and Sef. But he was dead sure of the difference.

In Seffie's and his case, it was Canaan who was the maniac.

And Seffie wasn't like Kate, growing up in a sound, loving family, having a core of strength and confidence. There was that thing about the wounded little girl in her.

"Have you considered that you are hurting her now, Canaan? Turning away from her love is costing you a lot. But it's costing her, too. Hurting her."

"*Kate.*" He scrubbed a hand through his hair, fighting an urge to beg the woman to stop. It was a long moment before he could speak. "She'll survive that, won't she? It won't be hard for her to find some damn doctor to love, who will love her just fine." He turned and sat facing her, his feet on the deck floor. "I could wake up with my hands on her neck, thinking I'm in Kandahar. *Believing* it. She won't survive that."

"You're so careful to not hurt her that you haven't fallen asleep with her, that you won't *be* with her, even though you love her. I don't think you have to worry that she'd come to harm from your hands."

He stood and shoved his fists into his jeans pockets. "It's not a chance I'm willing to take."

"You get to decide then? Josefina has no say in it?"

"I have to think in a few years she'll be grateful."

"I thought you knew her. I guess you don't really."

"I know that she's been hurt, Kate. She deserves something better in a man than I am."

Kate looked at Will and kept looking until, finally, she nudged him.

Will took his cue. "You're an idiot."

His wife lifted her brows and sighed out her impatience with the males of the species. "By which, Canaan, Will means this: You are a very good man. You have honor and loyalty. You love with your heart, and that means something important. You *see* people, and you do all in your power to protect those you love. Obviously, you'd sacrifice yourself to do it. So, *no*. Seffie *won't do* better in a man than you."

Canaan lifted his gaze from the floor enough to see Will silently nod his agreement. He wanted to howl with frustration. He couldn't discount the opinions of his friends, and it was a stone cold temptation to fall in with them.

But he couldn't take a chance with Sef. Of all the things he couldn't live with, hurting her would be the greatest.

"I'm gonna be out of town for a while," he said, no longer making eye contact. "There's a college kid home for the summer, from a farm up near Chelsea. I've arranged for him to help Joss out."

Will nodded again, letting Canaan know he'd check in on the moms. Will had a whole cluster of folks he looked in on and helped out when needed. He wouldn't hesitate to add Marta and Joss to the list. Canaan would have let it go at that and turned to the door, but Kate stopped him.

"Canaan." She got up and walked around the recliner to come close. Almost as tall as he was, she put both hands on his face and reached up a bit to kiss him. Softly, but on the lips, for a good little minute. "We love you. Don't be gone long."

Will was behind her now and reached out a hand to squeeze his shoulder. "Yeah. But don't think you get to keep kissing my wife when you get back."

"Are you awake?"

The sun was up, though it was barely after six. Josefina would have liked to have been asleep, but sleep hadn't come so easily to her the last couple nights. Not since Canaan had left her in his bed and then disappeared. *Really* disappeared. She'd searched. So, *yeah*, she was awake. "Canaan?"

He'd never called her before. They'd never spoken on the phone. She'd spent the last thirty or so hours thinking she might never see him or speak with him again.

"Can you come out?"

"Out?" Sef looked around her room, grounding herself. "I'm in my room. At the Hayeses."

"Yeah. I'm outside. Will you come out? Please?"

Sef moved the books she'd been working with aside and rolled out of bed. She had dormer windows to the front of the house—Leet's old room was essentially the attic of the Hayes's sprawling colonial.

She crawled onto a window seat and peeked out. The driveway was empty except for her hybrid. The Hayes's three-car garage was filled with their two Mercedes sedans and the old four-wheel-drive Subaru they used as their beater car. Sef pressed her forehead to the window. There, along the curve of road toward the distant neighbors, was Canaan's truck. And Canaan himself, leaning—though not exactly casually—against the tailgate. He had his arm bent, presumably with the phone still at his ear. She couldn't actually see it, because he wore a hat. A cowboy hat, leather, dark. Not light like the good guys wore. She could see strands of his hair, hitting sunlight beneath the shadow of the brim. He wore boots, too. Not the work boots he usually wore on the farm, but cowboy boots. He looked different, very western.

"I see you."

He could see her, too. At least it felt like his dark gaze connected with hers. She wouldn't know for sure, though, given the shadows from the hat.

"Yeah," he said, beginning to sound impatient. "Will you come?"

She closed the phone without answering and spent another minute looking out at him, considering.

She was afraid Canaan might break her heart, might be that thing she wanted that she wasn't, finally, able to get. She turned away and sat on the edge of the window seat, out of his line of sight while she thought about it.

As a rule, Sef was a practical sort. She'd learned the hard way not to rely much on others, not to expect them to love her or care about her or consider her needs. It wasn't something she ever fooled herself about. But she was uncertain about this particular situation.

She believed Canaan loved her. She was all but sure that spark she'd felt from the first moment she'd seen him had been mutual. That the careful, discreet way he watched her meant something. That the hot-sweet way they made love meant something, too.

Her heart was convinced about it. Intellectually, even, she was pretty confident he was holding back for some other reason. Not because he didn't love her.

Clearly, he wasn't ready for what she'd revealed on Saturday night. Maybe that had been a mistake, admitting her love and letting him know she dreamed of making babies with him. But she hadn't been able to resist. Seeing him at Sadie and Leet's, watching him hold Grayson against his chest, then take Vivienne so easily and make eyes at her, had tugged at her heart.

He'd been completely natural with them. He'd appeared to *enjoy* them.

A man shouldn't do that around a woman who loved him, unless he didn't care if she started getting ideas.

She'd gotten them.

He'd nearly put her off when she'd found him in his room. He'd seemed almost hostile at first, forbidding her to talk—that conversation she needed to have with him before Will had it—and instructing her to lie down on his bed or go away.

If that was an important clue about his state of mind, she'd lost track of it over the course of the next hour. His lovemaking that night had been so intense, so *connected*. She'd seen determination in his eyes, yes. Blatant, unbridled possession—that, too.

But love, really *love*, too. She was sure of it.

She probably should have bitten her tongue as soon as he'd turned away from her. It was beyond her, though, at that moment, to consider what it meant that, when she spoke, she was talking to the back of his head. It really didn't compute, given the way he'd made love to her. The way he'd *loved* her.

Well, she couldn't change it, couldn't go back to that moment and do it over. She probably wouldn't choose to anyway. Whatever she faced with the somewhat grim figure looming out there at his truck, she may as well face it now.

She spent a minute in the bathroom, not at all concerned that he should have to wait. There was no advantage in it to face him with teeth and hair unbrushed and looking like she just rolled out of bed. In fact, she paused as she reached for yesterday's jeans and reconsidered. There was nothing wrong with making sure he saw what he was turning down.

She chose a pair of short, tight-fitting blue jean cut-offs and a white cotton eyelet blouse that tied above her waist and looked pretty suggestive over the translucent, nude little bra she wore. She added a touch of lipstick and a little eye makeup and slid her feet into wedge sandals.

He had plenty of time to look her over when she stepped out the front door and walked to meet him—she didn't hurry about it. His jaw was flexing in a very satisfactory way when she got close. She stopped a couple feet away and waited. He'd left her alone on Saturday night and disappeared God knew where. He'd rousted her out of bed at six o'clock in the morning. He could damn well speak if he had something to say.

Apparently, he got the message, though it took him a long minute while frustration and fire warred in his eyes. It was an interesting effect and a little scary, those nearly black eyes shooting flames from under the shade of his hat. "I wanted to let you know I'm leaving the area for a while."

Well. Could we be any vaguer?

Sef was pretty sure she was supposed to be grateful that he'd gone out of his way to let her know. Like the chances were fair that he'd have left without speaking to her at all.

She stayed quiet, and that fire in his eyes burned a little hotter.

"You lied to me about that whole boyfriend deal."

Yeah, and she wasn't going to feel bad about it. "I told you I had a boyfriend and I don't. Do you really want to make a big deal about that?"

"Telling lies is hardly the way to start—"

She waited, but he wouldn't finish his sentence. All frustration, he stood straight—closer and taller—and put his hands on his hips.

She'd had enough. "Start what, Canaan? A *relationship*? Is that what we have? You can't even say the word."

"No. It's not what we have."

"It *is* what we have, you idiot. I love you. I told you one lie in order to have a chance with you. Don't pretend that's what this is about."

"I'm kind of tired of people calling me an idiot."

Seffie laughed roughly, a little mean. "Not alone in that

opinion, am I? Maybe you should start listening."

He took a hard breath, in and out, through his nose. Then he grabbed her forearm and held it against his chest. "Sef."

"No." She tugged her hand away. She couldn't tolerate his touch. Couldn't listen to the ugly words she knew were coming and touch him at the same time. "Say the words, Canaan. Tell me what your feelings for me are."

He'd let her go, opening his grasp on her abruptly, like she'd accused him of hurting her arm. Like he was going to do to her heart, whether he touched her or not.

"My feelings are that this can't work out between us, Sef. That you need to accept it and move on."

She huffed out a bitter laugh and shoved her hand against his chest. As though she was someone who expressed her anger physically. As though she had a chance in hell of moving him.

Still, she was close, up under his hat, facing those black eyes. "Those aren't your feelings, Canaan. That's only what you want to think, what you think you should think. Tell the truth. Look me in the eye and tell me you don't love me."

He did exactly what she told him to do. He said the words. But his mouth went grim and the fire in his eyes died first. "I don't love you."

Sef pushed away and turned her back on him. But she said one word first. "Liar."

He didn't speak again. Arms crossed beneath her breasts, as though she could guard herself from this pain, she listened to his footsteps. Boots on gravel. Then tires, as he opened and then closed the door of his pickup and drove away.

CHAPTER SIX

"Hey, Mom."

Carlie Liberty straightened at the kitchen sink, her back still to him. Unlike all his growing up years when she'd complained about the noise he made coming and going, he'd let the porch screen door close silently behind him.

Her sandy braid—largely gray now—still reached down her back to her waist. She wore boots and a plaid shirt tucked into her jeans. She was still fit and strong. Though she spent most of her work time in the kitchen—there were a lot of folks to feed—it wasn't all that unusual to find her out in the fields, riding tractor or horse, fighting flood or blizzard or whatever other hell nature dredged up, along with the men.

He'd caught her alone. It was July Fourth, and he saw the family still got together for a big picnic. Aunts and cousins were outside setting up the tables with red, white, and blue cloths and paper plates and napkins. Watermelons sat cooling in the shade of the old oak. Some kids were churning ice cream out there, the cold, sweet topping for his mom's famous strawberry and blueberry flag cake that sat ready on the kitchen counter.

They'd all raised their heads and watched as he drove onto the ranch, from the first cattle guard to when he pulled up into the yard amongst the family pickups and station wagons. Like country folk, they hadn't bothered to hide their interest when he climbed out of his truck, sent them a nod and a lift of his hat, and walked into the house without knocking. Like he belonged there.

But nobody had recognized him. His truck was new and relatively high-end—his single big purchase made from royalty payments. He was decently dressed and groomed, and walked in a way one wouldn't notice his missing foot.

The last these people had seen of him, he'd been an angry mess. His beard and hair were long and unwashed, his clothes filthy. He'd refused to wear a prosthesis, preferring to barge around carelessly and furiously on crutches, making sure everyone around him was fully aware of the damage done to him. He was drugged or drunk most of the time, his temper short and punishing.

It would take some time for all of them to get over it—them, their legitimate disgust and suspicion, him, his shame and regret. If it happened at all.

But Carlie Liberty was made of stern stuff. She reached aside for a kitchen towel and dried her hands with her back still to him. Her gaze was fixed out the window, but Canaan was sure her mind was somewhere else—rocking him to sleep as an infant, catching him in her arms with his first toddling steps, sending him off to his first day of school...

Telling him, the last time she saw him, that he'd never make her not love him, no matter what he did.

Her eyes were wary when she turned, but her smile was determined. He assumed it was the fact that he looked decently human when she saw him that had her breath coming out in a little glad cry. She covered her mouth to hold back the next one, but that didn't stop the tears from filling her eyes. In another second, her arms were lifted and open and her feet were bringing her close.

Canaan met her halfway, in the middle of that kitchen, the heart of the home he'd known as a child. A handful of inches shorter, she fit against him with her head tucked into his shoulder. Those strong arms held him just as he held her, and he could feel both her lips and her tears against his shirt.

He smiled as she mopped off a little, rubbing her cheeks into the fabric of his black tee. It wouldn't do to let him see serious tears.

Then she lifted her head to look at him—inspect him. She ended with her gaze deeply into his, and her hands clasping his face.

"You're better."

He nodded. "Yeah. Not perfect, though." Not complete, was more the case. Since the pieces of his heart were scattered on the road up there in New Hampshire.

He'd kicked himself every mile of the way to Cheyenne County for showing up at the Hayes' place like he had. He'd been right the first time, when he'd left Josefina in his bed and walked out with the thought of never seeing her again. That would have been better for her—giving her nothing to hope for, no opportunity to read the lie in his eyes when he told her he didn't love her.

Better for him, too, to not have to watch her disappear in his rearview, her back turned in those cut-off jeans and little top that showed more than they hid and made him burn to touch her. To not see her hold herself rigid, too proud to cry in front of him, but not so strong as to keep him from knowing that tears were falling.

He was way not perfect. And he was every bit the idiot both she and Will—the two in the world who knew him best—had called him.

His mother huffed and patted his cheek. "Well, perfect's not a standard we hold to around here. I'm so glad you're home."

He knew she wanted to ask if he was staying. And that she knew enough not to. He nodded his head toward the picnic outside. "Looks like I have the chance to greet the whole family. Where's Dad? And Bonnie?"

His sister had married into local law enforcement and started a brood of towheads that had gotten as far as four that he knew of, though he wasn't convinced she and Henry were done. She worked part-time as a nurse, but brought the kids and helped out at the ranch pretty often. The two were serious parents, all about raising their children well, so she worked her shifts around Henry's job with the county sheriff's office.

The last time Canaan had seen Henry, his brother-in-law had a strong grip on his shoulder and was giving him the option of leaving the county or face having to call his mother to come bail him out of jail.

"Bonnie took a bunch of the kids down to the creek for a swim. Your dad and uncles are out working on the irrigation in the southeast corner. They'll be coming in soon."

Canaan nodded. They'd have the picnic and then all pile into vehicles and form a convoy into St. Francis for fireworks.

He thought of all those he had to face and knew his sister would be the easiest. "Maybe I'll go help Bonnie haul the kids out of the creek in time for dinner. Is there anything you want me to do here first?"

Carlie patted his cheek and stepped back, willingly supporting his plan to ease his way back into the family. "I'm good. I have lots of help. You go on."

"Henry's not here yet?"

She gave no sign of knowing why he cared, but Canaan wasn't fooled. There wasn't much that happened in the Liberty family that the matriarch didn't know about. "No. His shift ends at four, so it will be a little bit."

"All right." He leaned down and kissed his mother's cheek. "I'll see you soon."

"Canaan?"

He paused and lifted a brow, waiting.

"Colleen may be here today. She joins us sometimes for get-togethers."

Ah. Back in another life—in high school, before the army—Colleen had been his sweetheart. "Is she still married?"

His mom shook her head. "No. That didn't last. I think she knew it was a mistake even as she did it."

Canaan nodded. There was another thing he had to atone for.

Colleen had been the best of innocence, bright and sweet. She'd lived in town, daughter of a librarian and Canaan's high school history teacher. In the bed of his family truck, he'd gotten his fingers on all of her best places and his mouth on a couple of them, but nothing more.

She'd promised to wait when he'd shipped out, but she was young. Like the girl she was—and *should* have been, she was only eighteen—she'd started dating Caleb Parker while he was gone.

The first time he'd come back, he'd raged at her.

The last time, he'd come close to breaking Caleb's jaw.

He stepped out to the porch and stopped to roll his shoulders. There was no reason to think coming home would be easy.

Out the screen door again, Canaan considered. He could sneak around back and avoid the crowd under the oak, but he had to face them sometime. And it could be that the women would be a little more willing to forgive. He'd never tried to slug any of them while he was in the midst of a drunken rage.

He hoped.

So he circled the porch to the side of the house. He took his hat off as he approached the group at the tables. The kids eyed him but kept at their activities. The women all went silent and watched him close in. He made eye contact and stopped at the first bit of careful warmth he found.

"Aunt Betsy. How ya doin'?"

His father's youngest sibling and only sister had always had a soft spot for him. She nodded and smiled as she confirmed his identity. "Canaan! You're looking mighty handsome."

She lifted her arms and he stepped into them, in his mind blessing her open heart. "And you're looking hot."

She laughed, unashamedly pleased at his words. There were only a dozen years between them, and they'd carried on a teasing flirtation through his adolescence. His heart had suffered a little bruising the day she married Marty Shea. And it was no coincidence that Canaan had followed Marty's bootsteps into the Army Rangers.

Marty hadn't come home from Afghanistan. Betsy had loved him hard, and as far as Canaan knew, she was still alone.

Her hug was warm and long and, he was sure, filled with relief. When she stepped back, she gave him a surreptitious wink and turned to face the other women—older and presumably less willing to forgive. "Pamela, Tammy, Michele—look who's here. Canaan looks great, doesn't he?"

Pamela was his father's aunt. Tammy and Michele had married the other two Liberty brothers. Pamela was old as dirt, and Tammy and Michele were significantly older than Canaan's mom and dad. As he remembered it, they'd all stopped thinking he was cute about the time he turned six.

Now the looks he got from them were sour enough that he had to suppress the urge to sniff his pits. Manning up, he went to each with a greeting, gave a small hug, and received a lukewarm one in return. They spoke a little about the weather and Independence Day traditions and grandchildren. None of them hid their relief when he said he was going down to the creek to give Bonnie a hand.

Betsy tucked her arm in his and invited herself along. As soon as they were out of hearing distance, she started laughing. "It was feeling a little chilly back there. Those women surely do hold on to their memories."

"They have a right to."

"No they don't." She said it with no hesitation, with such positive certainty that he wanted to stop and kiss her. "You came back from that war wounded, in more ways than one. They should be grateful you came back at all."

Unlike some.

Canaan had a moment where it was hard to breathe. Then she nudged into his shoulder.

"What is this?" She gestured to his legs as he walked steadily down an old tractor path. "Did they learn how to grow you a new foot?"

He smiled. "No, but they gave me a decent prosthesis. And I stopped being too stupid to use it."

She hugged his arm. "I'm so glad you're home. Bonnie will be happy to see you, and I'm sure your mother cried happy tears."

"She did."

"It won't be so easy with Jake."

"I know."

Jake Liberty was a hard man. Canaan's father wasn't mean. He'd never laid a hand on his children in anger, and he was, to this day, goofy in love with his wife. Vulnerable to her, he generally let Carlie soften his harder edges.

But he'd grown up poor, doing a man's work from the time he was ten, having to fight for respect that didn't necessarily come easily to a man whose father had come from the reservation, whose white mother had married beneath herself, as folks saw it in those days. It was Jake's Choctaw blood that had begotten Canaan's dark hair and eyes.

That was the heritage that had formed the man Jake was. He set hard standards for manhood, and in the last years, his son had failed to live up to them.

Everyone knew it. Jake Liberty wouldn't love a son he couldn't respect.

Canaan couldn't change the past, and he couldn't control his father's feelings. One day at a time, he reminded himself as they walked. Sometimes it came down to one hour, one minute at a time.

The Liberty ranch, as it had been cobbled together over

time, straddled the South Fork of the Republican River. Several small tributaries cut through the land, though many of them would be dry in another month. One near the house was bigger than others and some distant generation of Liberty children had dammed it up to form a good swimming hole.

Or perhaps it had been a group of desperate adults, determined to survive on their homestead, who built the little dam to ensure vital water for themselves and their stock.

Either way, generations of Liberty children had now learned to swim there, wading in or diving from a small dock. Young men had wooed their girls there. Some had proposed. And if certain winks or shy smiles meant anything, more than a Liberty or two had been conceived there.

Canaan had great memories of it—waiting for sunrise in the cool chill, as mist came off the water and the call of tanagers and wood pewees signaled daylight. Nights lying on the deck, feeling afloat in a sea of stars while frogs peeped and croaked and prairie dogs rustled. Splashing into the creek while the summer sun beat heat into his browned skin, or, in winter, slicing over it on skates, playing pond hockey with his cousins.

He remembered laughter, and he heard it now as he and Betsy approached. They paused to enjoy the view as they came over the rise.

Canaan's sister Bonnie stood thigh deep in the water. She had a water-winged three-year-old on her hip and was stretching a hand out to another kid, a bit older, splashing fairly ineffective swim strokes in front of her. Twenty-eight and the mother of four, she would pass for twenty-one. She was tan and lean and, in her really quite little string bikini, could have held her own on any trendy California boardwalk.

Two boys of about eight—one was hers, Canaan figured, and the other a cousin's son—practiced dives off the dock. A small cluster of girls with buckets and shovels played in the sand that was brought in by dump truck from Lake Michigan every few years. It was an indulgence for the children that bespoke the success of the ranch.

The girls' chatter fell to a stop when they saw Betsy and Canaan. At the silence, Bonnie turned. It took her a minute to recognize him. That minute was beginning to bother him. It reminded him of how far over the edge into hell he'd gone, that those who'd known him all his life needed a moment to relate who they saw now to who he was the last time he'd been there.

Thankfully, when her confusion cleared, Bonnie's face lit up. "Canaan!"

"Hey, Sis."

She grabbed the hand of the would-be swimmer and tugged him ashore. She left both him and the toddler on her hip with the girls and came to him. Cupping his ears, she pulled him down for a kiss and then squeezed him into a hug. "You look great, Nin-nin."

He grinned into the pleasure of the hug and her near-forgotten, two-year-old name for her little baby brother. He'd always counted himself lucky that it wasn't one of those nicknames like Rascal and Cowboy—two of his cousins—that had stuck.

She stepped back to look at him a bit more, her hands on his arms while he rested his on her hips—there really wasn't anywhere that he could touch that wasn't bare skin.

"You going to behave yourself this time?"

"Your husband let you run around naked like that? Isn't there some law he's supposed to uphold about that?"

"You answer my question, and I'll deal with my husband."

He could see now just a little bump and so he spoke in a drawl. "Looks like you *been* dealing with him." He kissed her again with an extra squeeze for the pregnancy and then turned to bring Betsy into the circle. "And yeah, I'm going to try to behave. I figured out last time that Henry gets a little cranky if someone calls him out of your bed to come haul me out of county lock-up."

She quirked her brow at that, but stayed wrapped arm-in-arm with him as she turned to watch the kids. "Have you seen Dad yet?"

"No. He's out working on the irrigation."

"These years have been hard on him, Nin."

"Yeah. I'm sorry for it, Bonnie."

Betsy had her arm around him from the other side. "What helped, Canaan? What got you better?"

He sighed. "It's a long list. Treatment through the V.A. Exercise. Tai chi. Goats. A couple of lesbians. Writing. Friends. All those things, and time."

Betsy and Bonnie both leaned around him to make eye contact with each other and spoke at the same time.

"Goats?"

"Lesbians?"

It was time for a strategic retreat. "Ma said I should help you corral the kids and bring them in for dinner."

"Yeah, don't think this is over. I recognize an evasive maneuver when I see one. And, what do you say, Betsy? You get the idea he left something out?"

Betsy was game. "You mean, like a woman?"

Canaan drawled again. "I mentioned the lesbians."

Bonnie laughed. "Uh-huh." Then she clapped her hands. "Come on, kids. Time for us to get going."

By the time they got back to the house, the crowd around the picnic tables had filled in. The men were back from the field—Cowboy and Rascal and their father Kyle were just arriving from the direction of the bunkhouse, where they'd obviously showered. Canaan's father and the other uncle—Rand—had likely done the same in the house.

Like the other men, Jake wore his go-to-church clothes—new Wranglers, his good boots and hat, and a plaid western shirt with pearl snaps. He had his hand on Carlie's shoulder when he spotted Canaan among the entourage from the creek.

The man always stood ramrod straight. It shouldn't have been possible for it to look like he straightened more when he caught sight of Canaan, but he did. Stiff and unbending, one might say.

Except for a few of the younger, oblivious kids, everyone's attention focused on the two men. A dozen feet away, Bonnie and Betsy stopped and let Canaan walk on alone, though they both gave him a little pat of encouragement. He was grateful as he could be for it.

He stepped close to Jake, facing him, but not close enough to touch, then gave a nod. "Dad."

"Son." Jake was a couple inches taller than Canaan, but narrower. They probably weighed about the same. But the old man was tough as nails, and Canaan was glad they'd never come to blows. Quite.

"You got your head on straight yet?"

Canaan nodded again. "Mostly straight."

"You hurt your mother when you were here last."

Yeah. And his father, too, though Jake wouldn't complain about that. Making Carlie cry would be the true sin. "I'm sorry for that. And she knows it."

"You think you can come back, dressed up and driving a nice truck, and it will all be okay now?"

"I don't know if it will be okay now or anytime in the future. I messed up, and I hurt people. I *was* messed up, but I'm trying to get better. If I did things that can't be forgiven, then when I leave, I won't be back." Canaan looked over his father's shoulder. Jake had moved to almost block his view of Carlie. The message was clear. If he meant to hurt Carlie again, he'd have to go through his father first. "I thought it might better to try than to stay away from here forever." He looked back to his father. "Maybe you don't agree."

His mother wasn't the little woman his father liked to pretend she was. Good thing, or she'd have lost herself in the marriage three decades earlier. She stepped forward and put her hand on her husband's arm. She stood fully beside him— no cowering behind for this woman. "There's nothing that can't be forgiven. Canaan, this is your home as much as you want it to be. You are always welcome and wanted here." She took another step so she could put a hand along his cheek for a little caress. Her voice firmed a little then, and she looked up at her husband. "Anyone who thinks otherwise can sleep in the bunkhouse tonight."

Canaan and Bonnie exchanged glances and suppressed smiles. There had been a couple famous occasions when the two were teens that Jake had found his pillow out in the bunkhouse.

Jake's cheeks reddened and he looked like he was chewing nails. But he'd never won an argument against his wife. Canaan felt movement next to him, and a warm hand slid into his. He knew who it was without looking. Colleen.

His dad had always had a sweet spot for Colleen, and there was no way he was going to face down both these women. He lifted his hat to her. "Colleen, girl." Then he looked dryly at his wife. "I'm sleeping in my own bed tonight, woman." He gave one more direct, challenging, don't-screw-up look to Canaan before he turned to the crowd. "Aunt Pamela, I hope you brought your cornbread. I've been looking forward to it all week."

Everyone took that for the signal it was. Folks started filling plates, the older ones making sure the younger ones got what help they needed. There was, indeed, Pamela's cornbread, Tammy's big crock of pulled pork, and Michele's pan of short ribs. Talk was quiet at first, but within a few minutes, it began to sound like a normal family gathering.

Canaan watched from where he stood, aware in the extreme of that hand in his. Finally, he turned to the woman at his side. She'd leant a hand in the confrontation with his father, and he appreciated the gesture.

"Hello, Colleen."

"Hi, Canaan. It's great to see you looking so good."

He let his gaze drift over her. She wore a light summer dress with a fitted bodice and a skirt that fluttered with the breeze and caressed her legs. She'd filled out, with more curves now than he remembered. Her eyes were only a couple inches below his. She was taller than—just taller.

"Thanks. You look good, too. I'm...pleased you're here. Mom said you come by some."

"*Surprised*, you mean? I enjoy it here. I always liked the ranch. And your mom and I have become friends of a sort. She's given me some of her recipes."

He looked at her in question. "Yeah?"

"I took over May Belle's bakery. I've made it a little coffee shop with pastries and sandwiches at lunch."

The crowd around the food tables had thinned a little, so he put his hand on her back and directed her there. "Really? That's cool. Are you making a go of it?"

"I'm doing all right. It took a while for the locals to get over thinking you ought to be able to get a good cup of coffee for seventy-five cents. But I hooked them with my baking. Those are my Earl Gray cupcakes and Jim Beam pecan bars on the dessert table." She smiled up at him, a bit impish. "Folks don't usually get them for free."

Canaan looked into her eyes, feeling regret and a gentle wish that he could go back in time. "I'll be sure and try them. I'll probably have to take down a couple cousins to get my share."

They'd filled their plates and turned toward the seating tables. He walked her to where Betsy and Bonnie sat across from each other. Colleen sat next to Bonnie. Though there was room beside her, Canaan walked around the table to sit with Betsy.

It was a big table, and Uncle Kyle and Aunt Tammy sat there, too, with Rascal and his wife and Cowboy and a couple of his kids. Betsy leaned across Canaan to talk with her sister-in-law, and Bonnie asked Cowboy about how his wife's honey business was going, and pretty soon the company was relaxed and comfortable. Canaan could sit quietly or join the conversation as he wished, and could feel nearly fully comfortable doing it. After a while, even his Uncle Kyle included him in his comments.

Later, Colleen got up to pass her desserts around. It was probably a good business move, but Canaan couldn't help but notice how she brought them to him first. He tried them both and gave her honest praise—she surely knew her way around a dessert menu. Still, he saved room for flag cake and ice cream.

He'd just set his fork down in surrender when, across the table, Bonnie's eyes lifted. It got a bit quiet around the yard, so Canaan was pretty sure he knew who stood behind him. Awkwardly, tucked in between Betsy and Rascal on the fixed bench of the table, he turned and stood up.

Henry didn't give him a lot of space, so in the end, they were face-to-face a meager handful of inches apart, gazes locked in a silent pissing match. Henry was a big man—he'd played college football—and didn't mind using his size to intimidate. No doubt it worked for him pretty well on the job.

Canaan knew something about combat and, by and large, didn't care how big a man was. But Henry had been decent to him when he'd first started coming around to see Bonnie, plus he'd seen Canaan at his worst and put himself on the line to get him out of a jam.

He owed the man. Henry had every right to act just as pissy and mistrustful as he wanted to.

Apparently, Bonnie didn't think so. "Hey, babe. Where's my kiss?"

In the end, Henry crumbled. Canaan saw the amused chagrin in his eyes first and then heard the heavy sigh. The man nodded once, said, "Liberty," and then walked around the table to his wife. Canaan figured the kiss he got was a bit more than the usual greeting—a reward bestowed on his behalf.

Henry squeezed in beside Bonnie, and Carlie brought him a plate of food—another reward, another debt owed.

Colleen was back when Canaan sat again, and the conversation at the table resumed. If Henry kept a steady eye on him, at least it felt watchful rather than critical. As dinner ended, Henry gave him orders couched as an invitation to join him for fishing in the morning.

Dinner and clean-up ended in time for the crowd to make it to the fairgrounds well before dusk. Kids took dogs and balls and disks, men carried coolers and lawn chairs, and women bundled up babies and blankets. St. Francis was a small town, and folks spread out on ranches didn't get to see a lot of each other. The Fourth was a big social event.

Canaan's oldest nephew and Cowboy's son begged a ride in his truck. He caught the look in Colleen's eyes and knew she'd have done the same thing. It was a bit of a relief to have an excuse not to offer it.

Belted in next to him, Calvin and his buddy Sam chattered the whole trip. Canaan's most important possessions—his guitar and *bō* staff—were visible, the one in the back of the cab, and the other secured in the bed. The boys were interested in both, and by the time they got to the fairgrounds, they'd come to an arrangement. The boys would wait for a demonstration of the staff back at the ranch the next day if Canaan agreed to play a couple tunes before the fireworks started.

Back in that other life, Canaan had played in a band. Though not great, his voice was decent, and he knew how to pick. The group had fallen apart when he joined up and the lead singer had headed to Austin.

It was less than ten years since Canaan had left home, but it felt like a lifetime since he'd sung in front of any of these people. In front of anyone besides a bunch of goats, in fact. Still, at the boys' insistence, he pulled his guitar from its case and let them tow him into the midst of the Liberty clan.

Making as little of it as possible, he edged his butt onto a chair and started strumming. He played quietly, making eye contact only with Cal and Sam. Folks were visiting, wandering from one group to another, but it wasn't long before he got a little attention. Eventually, with a mischievous look, Betsy walked up and nudged his boot with her toe.

"Play louder," she said. "And sing."

He looked around at the faces that surrounded him—family, friends, and strangers. He knew it would please his mother if he played and likely displease his father. Please Betsy and her little posse of girlfriends, and likely displease a bunch of others.

What the hell, he thought. If music didn't make him any friends, probably nothing would. He couldn't compete with Faith, but he surely knew his way around the song she'd made famous, so he let go with it.

Betsy nudged her friends. "He wrote that, you know." She said it with plenty of volume, and he could see others spreading the word. He caught his mother's eyes and could tell that she already knew. And was proud.

By the time he finished that song, most of the Independence Day crowd had circled around. By the end of the next one, he had another guitarist and a fiddler playing with him. The kid on the guitar really could sing, so he took over the vocals. The crowd had plenty of requests, and there was a little boot scootin' going on before it was over. His parents danced—it was Carlie who made that happen—and Bonnie and Henry, and Betsy with her group of women were shaking some bootie.

That bunch drew a whole lot of male attention.

Colleen had stuck close, but when Wade Nightingale came and asked her to dance, she put her hand in his.

They kept it up for more than an hour, ending only when the first big boom signaled the start of the night's real show. Folks hurried back to their blankets and chairs. Canaan nodded his acknowledgement to his impromptu band partners, but he didn't engage with them.

He already knew he'd be leaving.

Canaan committed to staying on the ranch for two weeks. He told Carlie first, so she wouldn't be fussing about whether he was staying or going. As expected, she soldiered up and told him she wanted whatever was best for him. He went fishing that first morning with Henry, and a couple more after that, and they got to a point where they were comfortable and enjoyed each other without really having to talk at all. Not so with Bonnie, who had to beat to death every reason he should stay and then cry a bit when she finally accepted that he would go.

He worked some on the ranch with his dad, but that never got easy. He spent more time at the house; his mom had conveniently decided it was time for a fresh coat of paint on the windows and shutters. He worked out with the staff and gave a couple lessons to Cal and Sam and some of the other kids.

Colleen had told him that first night to come by her shop and she'd feed him lunch. He put it off for a week and then drove into town late enough that he could be sure the lunch crowd would be past.

Sure enough, she was behind the counter, alone in the place, when he went in. She smiled, but took a good, measured look at him. Gesturing to a table, she said, "Have a seat. I'll make us some lunch."

She fussed at it more than she needed to. Before she joined him, she'd set croissant sandwiches on the table, plus some pasta salad with chunks of bright-colored peppers, a small bowl of fruit salad, and spears of asparagus wrapped in prosciutto.

"Thank you, Colleen," he said when she finally sat down with him. "That's more than enough. And it looks delicious."

They ate in silence until all he was doing was stabbing bits of fruit and taking them to his mouth with a fork. She kept her gaze on his, seeming to wait for him to start saying whatever it was that needed saying.

"I saw you dance with Wade the other night."

"Yes. We've been seeing a little of each other."

"I always liked Wade. He's a good man."

They'd played ball together in high school—all seasons, all sports. Wade was a superb athlete, and Canaan was pretty sure he'd taken a football scholarship somewhere in Texas. More importantly, a couple years back, Wade Nightingale had saved Canaan's ass when he'd been drunk down at the

Long House bar and goading a bunch of bikers into giving him a beating. It had taken a surprising amount of taunting to get the bikers mad enough to fight a cripple. Wade had held back, letting Canaan act like an asshole, until the very last minute.

That had happened a couple days before his brother-in-law had given him the bum's rush out of town.

Colleen nodded and lifted a shoulder. That wasn't a thing he knew how to interpret.

"You and Caleb didn't have any children?"

"No," she said. "Caleb wanted to, but I knew it wouldn't fix what was wrong with us." She paused for a minute, biting into an asparagus spear. "Wade has a four-year-old son his ex-wife left him with." She looked him over while she finished the asparagus. "Wade brought her back from U.T. Maybe you'll run into her someday. She's in Nashville, singing her little heart out."

Canaan remembered then that Colleen was always certain she knew what was right for everyone.

"Is it serious between the two of you?"

She twisted her fingers through strands of blond hair. "I think it could be. I also think it wouldn't take much for me to love you again."

Canaan wasn't surprised to know it, only to hear her say it so plainly. He met her gaze and spoke slowly. "I'm in no kind of shape to love a woman right now, Colleen."

Her gaze traveled down, taking in as much of him as she could see with the table between them. "You look in pretty good shape to me."

He took a breath in and let it out slow. This woman had found some gumption she hadn't had as a girl. "If I was in that kind of shape, there's a woman in New England I should be with."

"*Should be*? Because she loves you?"

"*Would be.*"

"Because you love her?"

"Maybe."

"Then you shouldn't be here, you idiot."

Canaan sighed. He wished he could get done hearing that from people who were supposed to know and love him. "That seems to be the prevailing opinion."

"If you don't go to her soon, I'm going to assume she's not the one for you."

He nodded. "I'm leaving next week." If he hadn't known it before, he surely did now.

"All right then." She stood and filled her hands with dishes. "I wish you well, Canaan."

CHAPTER SEVEN

"I shouldn't have had that last cup of coffee."

Josefina looked up at Trevor and smiled. Somehow, this sweet young man had become her friend. When she'd started medical school, Seffie had bonded with a small group of female friends. She felt most comfortable with other young women. She'd never really formed friendships with men except as they entered her circle by way of relationships with the women in her life. Like Leet and then Will. It was like that with Brandon, too, who was now going with her friend Heather. And Jenney's boyfriend Greg.

Trevor had worked his way into her group on his own. He'd had entrée as Greg's friend, but had made his own place in it. He was friendly with Shadow and Ashleigh, the two other single women left among Seffie's friends. And friendly with Seffie in a way that was intent enough to let her know that he was interested in more.

Like tonight, when he'd lingered as the party had broken up, waiting at her side while the others left.

It was her birthday, and the group had treated her to tapas and mojitos. She'd spent the earlier part of the day at Leet and Sadie's. Tino had helped bake her a cake.

"I don't think I can sleep for a while," he said now. "Would you like to walk around a bit? It's nice out."

It would be nice, Seffie thought. It was July, and the hot days cooled to comfortable evenings. Fourth of July celebrations had been rained out a few nights back, but the sky had been clear since then. Outside there would be cool air and a black sky dotted with stars.

And a patient, bright, sweet, and significantly cute young man to hold her hand as they strolled.

She couldn't say yes with a full heart, but she didn't say no. They walked around campus—old brick and ivy, the somewhat discordant modern buildings, the quad—and then strolled down to the river. The water was deceptively quiet on the surface—hiding a depth, Seffie knew, that made it dangerous.

Summer sounds surrounded them—frogs at the riverside, the first of the cicadas, music from the open windows of cars racketing across the bridge.

Trevor had taken her hand once they'd exited the restaurant, and hadn't let go. He'd been content, though, to walk quietly with her or chat about classes or the night. At the river, he'd settled her onto a bench and sat next to her. Close.

When they'd run through all the small talk she'd been able to summon, he sat quietly for a good long time. And when he spoke, she wished he hadn't.

"You've been unhappy since we came back from break. What happened?"

Seffie was silent for a moment. "It's...complicated."

"I know you have a son."

"Do you?" Seffie was surprised. She hadn't made any effort to deny Tino, but she didn't talk about him much in this part of her life either. Her girlfriends knew, but she didn't think they'd have told her story.

"A friend of mine from high school is a trainer for the Metal." Leet's football team. "He got me into a game last fall. We hung around after, and Tino was there with Leet's parents. I heard his birth mother was a med student." He squeezed her hand. "That would be you, right? I figure that's how you came to be living with the chairman of cardiology."

Seffie had met Dr. and Dr. Hayes when Leet came into Sadie and Tino's life. Aletha, in particular, had made an effort to get to know Seffie. She'd given Seffie a hand transferring to their Ivy League school, and eventually, secured her a place in medical school. And she'd welcomed Seffie into the Hayes home.

There was a story there, Seffie thought, behind Aletha's interest. She'd gently probed, but she'd never gotten the cardiologist to talk about it. Not even on the nights she'd seen Aletha Hayes partying and loose enough to grind hips with Bill Blade down at the Easy Rider.

"Yes. Tino's mine, though Leet and Sadie have adopted him. Sadie's had him since he was a baby."

"It must be rough. Having to give him up, I mean."

"Yes, it's rough. It's also good and right, Trevor." Seffie had to bite back her temper. Sweet, very innocent Trevor didn't deserve her bad mood.

"So...if it's not that, I'd have to guess it's about a guy. A guy other than me."

Seffie sighed, then she stood and walked to the river's edge. When she turned to face him, she had her arms wrapped around herself, like the cold she felt could be relieved in that way. "Yes. It's about a guy, and a thing between us that isn't going to work out."

Trevor had stood, too, and watched her from a couple paces away. "But it will keep this from working out, too, won't it? The thing that could be between us. It's not going to happen, is it? We can't even try."

Seffie shook her head, regretful. Trevor was sweet. He probably wasn't as uncomplicated as he seemed, but, for sure, he was a far sight less complicated than one Canaan Liberty.

"Who is it?"

"His name is Canaan. He lives on Tino's grandmothers' goat farm."

"He's a...goat herder?"

Seffie chuckled quietly at the description, so much an understatement for Canaan. "Yeah."

Trevor didn't hide his skepticism but lifted an arm and beckoned her into it. "Come on, Sef. I'll walk you back to your car."

They didn't speak at all then, but it was a reasonably comfortable silence. Perhaps, Seffie thought, they could be friends.

She guessed she'd been wrong, been a bit deranged even, to think that a warm, loving relationship would work for her. Certainly, it had been no lie, the doubt she'd had that she could participate in a healthy, loving sexual relationship. She'd fallen into hope, those weeks she spent with Canaan. They'd been together physically, and she'd enjoyed it, *adored* it. She thought she loved him, thought he might love her. Thought their love might be enough to truly heal her.

It had been a crazy sort of bliss, feeling fully human for the first time, like a woman who could have a whole life.

It wasn't wrong to think she deserved it. She'd had to give up so much. She'd lost her childhood to sexual abuse. She'd lost her *child*. Despite that doubting little voice in her head—in her heart, maybe, her core—she was entitled to better than she'd been dealt so far.

Seffie knew the odds, knew that many women with her history never recovered. That they struggled through one and then another abusive relationship, eventually passing their dysfunction down as a legacy to the next generation.

She'd hoped she was better than that. That she was smart enough, had had enough help. And for those few love-ly days, she'd felt victorious. Like she'd beaten the odds.

But Canaan didn't want her. And someone sweet and simple like Trevor, apparently, didn't really engage her heart.

What did that say about her?

The only obvious thing was that she'd been wrong. Her past was too much to overcome. She refused to accept that she wasn't worthy, that she was *unlovable*. People did love her, people with whole hearts and relationship skills and in-sight. Sadie loved her, and Marta and Joss, and even the Hayeses in their formal sort of way.

Tino loved her. And she was sure, certain to her soul, that his was an uncomplicated, pure love. Not the needy, desperate, twisted love of an abused child. That was a heart-break she'd avoided, a burden she didn't have to carry.

But she did have to accept this—she may be worthy, but she was *unskilled*. In the way that a child learns a language or to ride a bike, hardwiring the process into her plastic, youthful brain so the skill stays with her to adulthood.

Or not.

She was that adult who'd never ridden a bike as a child, destined to forever feel wobbly and uncertain. Only, the skill she lacked was the ability to engage in a healthy, loving, adult relationship.

So? She had a life. She had people and work that she loved. She would make that be enough.

Trevor must have heard her heavy sigh. He tucked her in a little closer as they crossed the street to her car. "Did you know that guy?"

Seffie looked up, surprised at the question. "Who?"

He nodded back to the corner—dark and shadowed and

empty as far as she could see. "He was across the street, watching like he knew us. Or you, I figured, since I don't know him." Trevor shrugged. "He's gone now."

"I didn't see him."

Driving back, Canaan took his time about it. He gave some thought to checking out the world's largest ball of twine, or the world's tallest something else, or...something. He wasn't quite ready to be back in Vermont, but he didn't want to be in Kansas.

He knew where home was now. It had been hard—leaving his mom, his sister, even Betsy. It hadn't been hard so much as *difficult* leaving his dad. There'd been tears from every one of the women, and hugs that were both warm and sad. From his dad, there'd been one more handshake, this one with maybe the smallest bit of thawing. But there was so much suspicion behind it, so much distrust.

Canaan could hardly blame him. Obviously, it would take years of rebuilding trust for things to ever be easy between them. In fact, it might never happen. Canaan had to accept that it might not and worked to resign himself to it. He could only do what he could do, could try to be a better man, to do the best he could. The rest, he'd have to leave to time. Time, and his mother's way with his dad.

His home was in Vermont now. He missed the farm and the damn goats. He missed Joss and Marta. They were like moms to him, in that way of love and acceptance despite all. But they knew him for what he was, accepted him as he was, without that huge, painful burden of disappointment and broken hopes.

He missed his friends—Will, with his quiet, easy apprecia-tion, and even Kate with—maybe despite—her sharp, sympa-thetic observation.

He missed Tino. Yeah, he really missed that little kid...

And Tino's mom?

Well, that was a tough one. Freaking tough. Sitting across the table from Colleen, Canaan had had to reconsider.

Apparently, he was man enough for Colleen—good enough, stable enough. Colleen had known him as a kid, at his innocent best. She'd seen him at his worst—the absolute depths of the hell he'd been in. Colleen didn't have Seffie's amazing brilliance, but she had a good, practical, even critical head on her shoulders. And she'd been evaluating Canaan not just as a man, but as a potential husband and father.

She hadn't found him lacking. It seemed she found him at least as good an alternative as Wade Nightingale. And if any man was to stack up pretty decently as a potential husband and father, it was Wade.

He felt like he ought to be able to rely on Colleen's judgment about it. More so, really, than his mom's or Bonnie's or Betsy's. Sure, each of them would hope for him to settle happily into a relationship with a woman, would want for him the fullness of life that came with a family. His female relations would naturally lean towards believing he was ready for it, capable of it. They'd believe it even against evidence to the contrary. They wouldn't be betting their futures on it, their lives, their bodies.

Colleen would have all those things at stake. And it appeared she knew how to look out for herself. A thumbs up from her meant something.

Was that enough? Could it ever be enough for him to risk it? Seffie was bright and sweet and fucking wounded. That hurt, vulnerable bit inside her scared the hell out of him. She was like an injured bird. To help, you had to know what you were doing, or chances were you'd cause more harm than good.

If there was ever a man who didn't know what he was doing—well, Canaan Liberty was head of that unhappy parade.

When he'd left the ranch, his mother had looked him in the eye and put her hand on his chest. "You have a good heart, Canaan. You can trust it. That's what I want you to do. Please, do that for me."

A well-meant instruction from his mother. A thumbs up from a prudent, fairly shrewd woman.

That's what he carried with him on the road back to Vermont.

If Sef had any sense, she'd find herself someone else, some equivalent of Wade in her world of brilliance and accomplishment. The way he'd left her, lying to her face, denying his feelings for her like the worst sort of Judas, she'd like-ly never want to see him again anyway.

And if she didn't, well, that solved the problem for him. One problem, anyway—that stone-cold fear of hurting her.

Not the other problem. The one about his own heart—how it might never be whole and happy without Josefina Claire.

So he drove himself home. He skipped the ball of twine, but he pulled his truck over every so often—at the view of a pretty farm, alongside a quiet creek. He hung off the tailgate or settled his butt on a fallen log. He plucked his guitar and wrote a couple songs. Love songs. I-done-broke-my-woman's-heart songs. All-I-got-left's-my-pickup-truck songs. Gonna-have-to-get-me-a-dog-if-I-want-somethin'-warm-to-sleep-with songs.

Josefina's mother, Gloria Alonso, had been sent across the river when she was fifteen. Her family needed the money from even the lowest wages she could earn on the other side of the border. So she stayed with an uncle in a small bed-room she shared with two cousins in Del Rio and worked with her aunt cleaning barracks at Laughlin Air Force Base.

Three years later, she was pregnant and living, unwel-come and unloved, with her husband's family on Staten Is-land.

Seffie never knew whether there was any love between Gloria and Senior Airman Robert Claire. By the time Seffie was old enough to remember, Gloria had burned her last bridge with Robert and his family. In Gloria's drunken and drugged ramblings, Robert ranged from the love of her life, in which Seffie was conceived amidst romance and tender-ness, to a predator who took advantage of innocent girls.

Either way, he'd married her and had no more sense than to bring her home to a family who would never accept her, a pregnant Mexican teen-ager. Eventually, before Seffie was old enough to remember him, he'd moved on. His family had maintained no commitment to either mother or child.

Nonetheless, the pattern had been set. If Robert Claire had been Gloria's first lover, her second was another airman, this time one on leave from Stewart. Later, she branched out—to other *branches*. Certainly, on the worst days and nights when Gloria was desperate for a hit, any man at all would do. But by and large, the men she attached to were military.

Seffie had to assume that Mateo Silva was the worst of the lot, though that might have been true only by virtue of her unfortunately close acquaintance with him. Mateo came into Gloria's life when Seffie was ten. Mother and daughter were living in transitional housing then, saved from home-lessness only by the Department of Social Services. One of Gloria's sisters had moved to Flatbush, and even she'd had enough of Gloria's disruptive, dangerous behavior. When Aunt Rosa finally tossed Gloria out, she'd offered to keep Josefina.

But no, Gloria needed her "baby."

Mateo came and went, but for several years he was a fairly steady figure in Gloria's home. Sometimes things were better when he was there. He'd lost vision in one eye, and Army disability checks came once a month. On those nights, there were parties—big ones, at which Seffie was welcome, if only to keep the cooler stocked with beer and bowls of chips and salsa filled. Sometimes the party was just for two, when Mateo and Gloria sank into that dark place they went to with needles. Then, Seffie had to keep herself quiet and scarce.

Mateo had a certain charm. He could be sweet with Glo-ria, and with Seffie, too, if the mood took him. She remem-bered trips to the beach or the zoo, when there was a real sense of family. But he was volatile and mean—even vio-lent—when he was drunk.

Part of those years, Seffie spent with Rosa's family. If things were good with Mateo, Gloria would be happy to spend all of her time with him. For weeks or sometimes months, she'd send her daughter away. Seffie would bunk with her cousins and go to school with them. Those were the best, most stable times of her childhood.

But always, eventually, Gloria would crash. The drugs or alcohol became not enough to support her mood. Mateo left or edged into abusiveness. When that happened, Gloria would remember her baby and want her home.

And then, when Seffie turned thirteen, it was Mateo who

wanted her home.

Seffie had been aware the first time Mateo had seen her as something other than a nuisance girl. Gloria was at work. DSS had mandated job training and employment, and Gloria now very unhappily had a night shift job as a CNA.

Drunk or drugged, Mateo was dangerous, and Seffie knew to stay away from him. She hid in her room, studying for school, reading on the Internet. Her door had a lock and, most nights when Mateo was in a mood, that was enough to deter him. Sometimes he'd pound with his fist and, often, he'd holler out curses and disparagements. The headphones she used blocked some of the noise.

Usually, he was away when she first came home from school, so she'd raid the cupboards, such as they were, for her dinner before she locked herself into her room. She wouldn't go out again until he'd drunk himself to sleep.

That particular night, she miscalculated. Mateo had been quiet for long enough that she ventured out to the bathroom and then stopped in the kitchen for the nearly empty jar of peanut butter. When she turned back to her room, she saw his eyes glittering, watching her, from where he was laid out on the couch.

She had breasts and curves by then, and she knew enough to shudder at the way he watched her.

A few weeks after that, on the night of her thirteenth birthday, the lock on her door wasn't enough to keep him out.

Gloria must have seen it—the broken lock, the splintered wood of the door casing. She never mentioned it. And the next time Seffie escaped to Rosa's, Gloria was there the following morning, heavy makeup not quite covering her bruised face and bloody lip, to fetch Seffie home.

Seffie always wondered what would have happened if, on that first morning, she'd gone to her Aunt Rosa and clung. And why she hadn't.

Years later, she understood the psychology of an abused child, of one who grew up with the rocky, needy foundation of inconstant love. She knew how worlds were constructed in which children learned to expect no more than what they got.

But on that day, she hung her head, swallowed back

tears, and accepted her fate. She lived in hell for the next three years, until her pregnancy was so advanced that even neglectful, oblivious Gloria had to acknowledge it. Then, as though it was her fault, Seffie was banished from her mother's home.

Gloria's sort of maternal love was no great loss. And that day marked the last she'd seen of Mateo. All in all, it was a good day. One now seven years past.

Despite his substance abuse, Mateo had always stayed fit. He'd learned to box in the Army and still sparred sometimes in the years that Seffie knew him, even with his vision in only one eye. He was strong. And mean.

And so, when she saw him again, Josefina knew she was in trouble.

Canaan was sure Sef knew he was back. He'd seen Tino a couple of times and, God knew, that kid didn't stay quiet about anything. And, anyway, Canaan had made no effort to hide it.

Joss and Marta had welcomed him back quietly and with relief he could see in their eyes. They sat him down to feed him, and Joss had updated him on the farm and what needed doing next. They debated a little the idea of developing a small plant to make their own cheese—on a larger scale than Marta did sometimes for the kitchen—versus continuing to ship out the milk to be converted to cheese at the creamery down in Grafton. It was a conversation they'd had a couple times before.

That first night, Marta had stayed behind, waiting to be alone to ask him about Seffie. He didn't know what he was going to do about her, he told Marta in answer to her gentle question. Mostly, he said, he expected she'd want nothing to do with him. If she was dumber than he thought, or softer, well, they'd just have to see.

Those words earned him a mild scold, but it was a spade he had to call a spade.

Sef didn't show up at the farm for a suspiciously long time. If Tino, or Tino and Jace, spent a day at the farm, well, someone other than Sef provided the transportation. And when she did come, a couple weeks after Canaan got back, she kept to the house. When he saw her, he avoided going in to eat, until he realized that she was always gone by any mealtime.

But Tino was game as usual, and brought Jace along to help him goad Canaan about *bō* fighting lessons. They caught him one evening in the barn as he was working out.

Canaan had skipped dinner. He'd seen Sef bring the boys and, though he knew she'd be gone, he couldn't force himself to go into the house and be fit company.

A good workout was what he needed instead, though he could hear Marta in his head, chastising him, reminding him that he was wanted. Joss was in there, too, calling him an idiot and a coward.

It was August now, and hot, and he'd worked up a good sweat. It had taken a while before he could shut down Marta's and Joss's voices in his head, and even longer to suppress thoughts of Sef. He'd finally got to the quiet, that place of calm inside himself, so he didn't stop when he became aware that Tino and Jace had come to the open doors and watched.

Because of the heat, he'd stripped to only a pair of loose shorts. He knew what they saw—a man scarred and peg-legged, battling his inner demons. He heard their conversation—Tino's blunt curiosity about Canaan's prosthesis and Jace's matter-of-fact explanation.

Of course, they didn't have the sense to run. And after a few more minutes of it, he couldn't in good conscience leave them to process the whole deal on their own.

So he stopped, gave short shrift to a closing form, held the *bō* as a walking staff, and headed over.

Jace had grown in the couple years Canaan had known him, filled out with the muscle he'd need for the quarterback he yearned to be. He was taller than Canaan now, by an inch or two, and maybe wasn't done growing yet.

Still, he was a kid, and a good one. He didn't mind that Tino was clutching his shirt, tugging for attention.

"That's what I want to do," Tino told his big brother urgently. "He's going to teach me. Now, Canaan? Can we use the stick now?"

Canaan smiled a bit as he approached and shook his

head. "Wax on, wax off, little grasshopper," he said, mixing references that Tino wouldn't get anyway.

But Jace met Canaan's eyes and grinned before he looked back at Tino in response to another tug.

"What does that mean?"

"It means, first you learn more tai chi. Then you learn to fight with it. Then you learn the stick."

Canaan nodded, glad that Jace got it. That was the benefit of training for a sport, of learning discipline, of having a coach to mentor and inspire.

But Tino pouted. "You can't fight with tai chi."

"Sure you can, grasshopper. Watch." Canaan grinned, made Tino happy by handing him the *bō*, and took a couple steps back. He motioned at Jace. "Come at me. Go for a high punch."

Jace understood they were only making a point for Tino's benefit, but he was enough cocky kid to want to put something into it. So with decent body mechanics, bringing power from his legs, he took a couple steps and threw a good right.

Canaan deflected it, grabbed the kid's arm, turned, and took him down. He held him as he went, not quite dropping him into the dirt.

"What was that, Tino?"

"Cool!" was the response.

"Yeah, but what was it? What form?"

"Huh?"

He'd pulled Jace to his feet. "Again. Slow motion this time."

They repeated their actions, but Tino was still in the dark.

"Watch, grasshopper. Watch my motions. What am I doing?"

Canaan and Jace went through it again, and this time had Tino jumping up and down and pointing. "Repulse the monkey! Repulse the monkey!"

Canaan grinned. Anything that had a monkey in it was a favorite for Tino. He motioned to Jace again. This time, he deflected Jace's blow, then stepped in and pushed into his chest, backing him off.

Tino was quiet for a minute. "Grasp the bird's tail!"

They did a few more moves, and Tino got it. "White crane flashes wings! Snake creeps down! Cool! Now me! Now me!"

Schooling his face into honor for his opponent, Canaan faced Tino and nodded. Of course, all Tino wanted to do was whale away, but Canaan blocked the first blow and then held him steady, wrist grasped and hand into his chest, until he got his attention. "Try single whip," he advised.

Tino took a breath and found his discipline. He gave a decent execution of the form. Canaan blocked it but took a couple steps back. "Kick with right heel."

They spent an hour at it, with Jace taking a little instruction from Tino about the forms. By the time it was full dark, Canaan had lost his mad. His sweat had dried, his body had cooled, and so had his head.

When Joss came out to corral the kids into the house for bedtime, Tino asked if they could sleep in the loft of the A-frame, like they used to when Sadie had first brought them to live on the farm.

Canaan waited for Joss's response—a nod saying okay, another indicating it was his choice—before he answered. "Sure, if you'd like."

They raided Marta's kitchen for homemade root beers and snacks, which they then consumed on Canaan's porch. He carried a sleeping Tino slung over his shoulder up the ladder to the loft—one step at a time, leading with the right. He hit the sack himself, all but asleep before it occurred to him he hadn't stopped to worry about what would happen if he woke in a terror.

He was there when she walked to the bike rack. Mateo.

Sef was alone. She'd turned down Shadow's encouragement to join the group going for pizza and beer after class. Shadow had worry in her eyes and concern in the hug she gave when Sef declined the invitation. It was on the lamest of excuses—she'd biked to school, and so had to get home before dark. Both women knew there would be more than one freely extended offer of a ride if Sef stayed.

Sef knew that her friend had been watching her the last month, aware of her distress. So was Trevor—watching and aware. She'd even seen them talking together, Shadow and Trevor, and she was sure she was the subject of the conversation.

This wasn't her only lamely made excuse lately. Tino had been eager for another tai chi lesson following some session with Jace where there'd been "real fighting." He begged, and Sef sank to claiming she was too busy with school. It had gotten too hard to go to the farm.

She'd declined lunch in the quad with Shadow and Ashleigh, and a trip to the outlet mall with Sadie and Kate with equally poor excuses.

She'd spent two weeks studiously avoiding making more contact with Trevor than a nod and a smile.

She was glum and feeling sorry for herself. And alone. Apparently, that was what she was destined to be.

And so it made sense that she was alone now, facing Mateo.

By the time she saw him, she was only a few paces away. She hadn't been paying attention, wallowing instead in her little misery. Apparently, she'd lost her radar for him, that hyper-awareness that had saved her many times— though not enough times—in the past.

He looked better than he should. Mateo was several years older than Gloria, probably nearing fifty now. His slicked-back black hair showed no signs of gray. His skin was tanned, smooth, without the ravages that should have come with the years of substance abuse and hard living. He looked fit, strong.

Wearing dark sunglasses, an untucked cotton shirt, and plaid shorts, he leaned against the bike rack as though he belonged there. As though he might be visiting a college son or daughter, as benign as that, as random.

But it wasn't random. He was next to her bike; one of his sandaled feet pressed up against the tire.

"*Chica*," he said, in a tone that sounded friendly, normal. No one else would hear the taunt in it.

Sef turned around. She walked away, barely keeping herself from running. But she'd run if she had to, scream if she must.

She found Shadow and the group of third-years at the local pizza haunt. She got there without ever once turning around to see if she was followed.

CHAPTER EIGHT

Josefina spent a week not eating, not sleeping. She never rode her bike—as far as she knew, it was still locked to the rack on campus. She drove her car on the days she had classes, and varied the lot where she parked. As much as possible, she never went anywhere alone.

Most importantly, she never went to see Tino.

She saw Mateo almost every day. From a distance, she saw him at the bike rack again that next day, after riding to school with Aletha Hayes. She went by the hospital then and claimed a ride home with Nathan. One time he was outside the medical library when she walked out after a study session, making sure she was in the middle of the group. A couple days later, he was in the hallway, inside the building, when she left lecture—again, carefully surrounded by fellow students.

He watched her.

And he wasn't the only one.

Seffie was aware that Trevor watched her, too.

At the end of the week, he stopped her. He was in the same clinical group with her, and they were about to start their OB rotation. They'd had skills training, practicing maneuvers for OB emergencies in the simulation lab. When the class was over, Trevor stopped her with a hand on her arm and pulled her into the student lounge. He sat her down at a table in a corner far away from the windows.

He slid a chair over and sat facing her. "The man who's been stalking you is outside right now."

Seffie stood, meaning to walk away, but Trevor held her hands and nudged her back to her chair.

She tried one more evasion. "I don't know what you're talking about."

"He's the same man I saw the night of your birthday."

Seffie dropped her head. "Oh." *Oh no*, was what she really meant. That was two weeks before she'd seen Mateo. It
was the very day she'd been to Leet and Sadie's to celebrate
her birthday. The day she'd been with Tino. She'd been with
him in the days after, too. She'd taken him to the farm.
She'd picked him up from his summer arts program—he was
sketching trees, because Leet had told him a sculptor needed
to learn to draw.

She shuddered, and when Trevor reached out a finger to
her chin, raising her head, she knew she'd missed whatever
he'd said.

Patiently, quietly—steadily—he repeated it. "Who is he,
Sef? Do you need help?"

She shook her head.

"You've been driving your car every day, but your bike is
in the rack. It's in the same spot it's been for a week."

"The brakes need work. I've been meaning to put it in
the car to take to the shop, but I keep forgetting. I've been
busy, you know?" She tried for a smile, aware that it wob-
bled.

He was too smart to fall for it, and too concerned to let it
go. "He's stalking you. You're in trouble, Sef." Trevor leaned
closer, his fingers a gentle caress now. "Sef, is he Tino's father?"

Seffie leaned away from his touch and put her hands
over her face.

"He is, isn't he? He's the one who abused you. That's
what it would have been, right? Tino's what? Seven or eight
now? You must have been sixteen when he was born."

With a couple slow breaths, Seffie centered herself. Of all
things, it was Canaan's tai chi that helped her. She lifted her
head to meet that concerned gaze. "I might be in a little
trouble, but I'll handle it, Trev. I have a friend who's a—"

"A cop? The deputy who checked me out?"

"How do you know that?"

Trevor smiled a little, in a way that didn't reach his eyes.
"*Principles of Clinical Diagnosis*? Our first class together. Remember what we learned?"

Sef dug for her own smile. "The powers of acute observation?"

He nodded. "Was it you or Canaan who put him on me?"

Canaan. How much did Trevor know? Sef shook her head. "It wasn't me."

She could see Trevor liked that. "I'll go with you—to see him. The cop."

"Thanks, Trev. But no. I'll talk to him. I promise."

"Do you want me to get your bike? I can load it into my car, get it home for you."

That about undid her. "I love you, Trev."

"Yeah, yeah. What's the combo?"

Trevor took Seffie out the back of the building and insisted on walking her to her car. He stood and watched as she started it up and left the lot. But she wasn't even out of the village before she pulled to the curb and stopped.

She had to assume Mateo knew about Tino, knew where he was.

Sef hadn't seen her mother since before Tino was born. But her aunt Rosa had been with her those last weeks of pregnancy, and in labor, too. She knew about Tino, and so probably Gloria knew, too. And if Gloria knew, no doubt Mateo did as well.

After Leet and Sadie had married, Seffie had formally, legally, given up rights to Tino. On his birth certificate as well as on the parental rights relinquishment, the box for father contained only the word "unknown." Seffie had never named Mateo. And had hoped—really, *really* hoped—to never see him again.

She finally had to acknowledge that as a ludicrously childlike wish. She'd spent a week now hiding her head under the blankets, trying to convince herself the monster in the closet wasn't real.

Mateo was real. He was present—and had been for nearly a month now. He no doubt knew everything about her he wanted to know, including—*especially*—those things she didn't want him to know.

He probably wouldn't go away until he got what he wanted. No, not probably. *Definitely.*

Sef turned the car around and went back to campus. She parked once more, walked around to the front of the med school entrance, and found him.

He straightened from the brick wall he'd been leaning against when she walked up to him. The building had emptied now, and they were alone.

"What do you want, Mateo?"

"*Chica*." He raised a hand as if to touch her. As if it was a caress.

She batted it away. *Cloud hands*.

"What do you want?"

Above his sunglasses, a brow lifted. Yes, he might wonder if she'd grown up a little. If she wouldn't be as easy to manage as she'd once been.

He'd better freaking wonder.

He took stock for a moment. "I want to see you, Josefina." He said her name with Spanish inflection, and as though he was speaking to a lover. "And I want to see my son."

That last was said more severely. Like to make his determination plain.

"You have no son. At least not by me."

"You lie, and I know it. His name is Constantino. And you have given him to that midwife and her big shot football player husband. You gave my son to another man. I want him back."

"You're dreaming. Tino isn't yours."

Mateo lowered his glasses so he looked at her with his dark eyes, even that scarred one without vision seeming to see through her. To find that child inside who was at his mercy. "You had some other lover besides me?"

Lover. What a farcical description of what he'd been to her.

"Did you not know? Nine months before Tino was born, I went to a frat house at NYU. I got drunk and let some of the boys there use me. I did that several times during those years that you...that you forced yourself on me. As you might guess, I had a little trouble figuring out appropriate sexual behavior in those days." She leaned forward, into those cunning dark eyes. "*Tino is not yours*."

"You spin a good story. It will only take a DNA test to prove you as the lying little bitch that you are."

"Sure. Good luck with that. Go ask the football player for a little of his son's blood."

"Not his son. *My* son. I have legal rights."

Seffie scoffed. "You have rights you could claim only by admitting to a felony."

Mateo leaned back again, a man comfortably at leisure. "No charges were filed. You had until five years after you turned eighteen to seek legal action if you thought you had a case. How old are you know, Josefina?"

Twenty-three. And three weeks. She understood now why he'd shown up when he had.

"You must not have thought you had a case. Admit it, *chica*. You enjoyed my loving."

Appalled, nauseous, Seffie took a step back. "Go away, Mateo. You can't have Tino, and you can't have me. There's nothing for you here."

"Do you think they can keep him from me? Even the big shot? The boy plays at a farm with only women and a cripple. He goes to his little art class—Monday, Wednesday, and Friday from nine to noon. Soon he will go to school. *Chica*, I'll take him if I want him."

Seffie nearly smiled at his characterization of Canaan, yet another underestimation of the man. But Mateo's studied observations were too chilling. She tamped down her fear and clung to the one word he'd said that gave her hope.

"*If* you want him?"

"At the least, I should be compensated for my loss."

Ah, Seffie thought. Here was the point of this conversation. She should have guessed. "You want...compensation."

Mateo nodded. "You live in a fine house now—I've seen it. You drive a new car. You're doing well for yourself."

Seffie huffed. "I'm broke. The car and the room in the house are gifts, as is my tuition. I have no money, Mateo. None."

He wasn't deterred. "The midwife will pay to keep the boy. She has the football star's money."

Shaking her head, Seffie knew it was useless to try to bluff. Sadie would pay. Of course she would. "No."

Mateo slipped his glasses back on. "You talk with her. I'll have a bank number for you when I see you in a couple days. I'm thinking big numbers, *chica*. Lots of zeroes. We can make it easy that way. Or, we can negotiate ransom."

Seffie turned so she didn't have to watch him walk away.

Canaan had just showered off the grime of a day in the barn and his evening workout when someone knocked on his door. Wearing nothing but a ragged pair of cut-off sweats, he opened it.

A kid stood there. He wasn't a big guy, maybe five-ten, wiry like a tennis or squash player. He had sandy hair styled expensively and with some product, and teeny little glasses that announced his nerdiness.

But he gave Canaan the same once-over he'd been given, then met Canaan's gaze steadily. Canaan had to feel he'd been found lacking.

No, not a kid, not really. He had some stones.

He spoke first. "You Canaan?" It wasn't much of a question.

"Yeah."

"My name's Trevor. I'm a friend of Josefina's."

Ah. The would-be boyfriend. *The privileged little snot.* "Yeah?"

"She's in trouble."

Shit. Canaan stepped back and motioned him in. "Talk."

He walked a few paces in, over toward the windows, and turned to face Canaan. "There's been a guy watching her, *stalking* her, really. For almost a month now. I saw the guy before she did. It was a couple weeks before she caught sight of him."

Fuck. "I gotta dress. Follow me, and keep talking."

Trevor came along to the doorway of Canaan's bedroom. He crossed his arms over his chest and leaned against the frame. If he was awkward about seeing a guy strip down to nothing, it didn't show. A team sport then. He'd spent some time in locker rooms. Lacrosse, probably.

"Does she know him?"

"Yeah. And she's afraid. It's Tino's father. The guy who—"

"Got it." And *fuck* again. Canaan got himself into a black tee and black fatigues. He sat on the bed to shove his feet— one foot, one prosthesis—into socks and boots. "Where is she?"

"I put her in her car and sent her home." He glanced at

his pricey watch. "That was a couple hours ago. It took me a while to find you."

Goddammit. Canaan had to like the kid. *Okay,* the *man.* "Where's the skank?" He motioned and had Trevor following him out the door.

"He was waiting for her outside the med school. I took her out the back. Either he's still there, or somewhere else."

A little sass. Stones, and he wasn't an idiot either. They were striding towards the barn. He gave the guy a look, waiting for Trevor to return his gaze. "Thanks, man."

Trevor nodded. He waited until Canaan had opened the lock box that held the key to his gun safe and they were headed back to the A-frame before he spoke again. "You love her. Why are you being such an ass about it?"

Canaan sighed. But the guy wasn't making an accusation so much as truly asking the question. Canaan got the sense he liked to understand things. And he probably deserved an answer. Apparently, he'd been taking care of Sef better than Canaan had.

"I'm not exactly whole, you know?"

Trevor snorted a bit, a guy sound that somehow made Canaan trust him. "Because you're missing a foot?"

"No," Canaan said, and waited for the kid's eyes. "Not *only* that."

He was being measured again and found he didn't mind it so much this time. It looked like Trevor could see things.

"Yeah," he said. "Well, you're hurting her. So you should hurry up and get over it."

"Yeah. I suppose."

When they got back to the gun safe, he opened it up and handed the kid his Remington 700 with a good scope. He left the AR where it was. Then he knelt and fastened an ankle holster and gun on his good leg, a knife sheath to his prosthesis, and tucked a snub thirty-eight into the back of his waist. On a last thought, he grabbed his night vision gear.

He took the 700 back and said, "Let's go. We'll take my truck. Get out your cell and call Sef. Find out where she is."

She probably wouldn't answer Canaan's call. At least she hadn't, the one desperate night he'd tried reaching out. He loaded the rifle into his cross-bed box. When he got behind the wheel, he had his own phone out.

"Leet, where are you...? Is Sadie there with you...? Something serious is going on. Go upstairs and put your eyes on Tino right now... Do what I say, then call me back."

Will had his phone out by the time Seffie had finished her second sentence, out there on his front porch. She'd let him know she was in trouble. Tino, too.

He pulled her in, taking her into the living room even as he opened his phone. When he finished his short instructions to Leet, he took her to a tropical print sofa. "Sit," he said. "Do you want something? Wine, coffee?" He continued when she shook her head. "Maybe we should have Kate for this?" She nodded and he nodded back. Then he answered his phone. "Good. Lock down the house. I'm coming over there with Josefina." He looked at Sef. "Tino's safe. I gotta get a couple things. I'll send Kate down, but don't start without me." He smiled a little. "Okay?"

"Yeah, okay."

Seffie sat alone for a minute and tried to gather herself.

She felt better, already taken into Will's care and knowing that Leet was with Tino and would keep him safe. More than anything, she'd longed to go to Canaan. But this was better.

Kate came into the room a couple minutes later, bringing with her, of all things, a cup of cocoa. She handed it to Seffie and then sat down beside her.

Seffie had dressed for summer, for classes, like it was a normal day. She wore a collarless, sleeveless top and khaki shorts. The hot mug in her hands was remarkably comforting and the sweet scent soothing. So was the presence of the warm, bright woman next to her. By the time she'd taken in the heat and scent of the chocolate, Will was there.

He'd changed from a ragged tee and old board shorts to jeans and a polo covered by a light jacket. She guessed the jacket also covered a shoulder holster. He had a travel mug in one hand, and Seffie was sure it contained hot coffee.

"All right," he said as he took a seat across from her. "Fire away."

Seffie took a breath, looking from one to the other. And then to the tropical fish tank beyond Will's shoulder. "Tino was fathered by a man named Mateo Silva. He was my mother's boyfriend, in and out of the house from when I was ten. When I was thirteen, he started to—"

"Sexually abuse you," Kate finished for her.

Seffie swallowed. "Yes." She still had both hands wrapped around the mug, but she felt Kate's touch land gently on her shoulder. After a moment, she went on. "When Gloria, my mother, realized I was pregnant, she threw me out of the house. I didn't see Mateo again until a week ago, when he was waiting for me on campus after my last class of the day. "I didn't talk to him then. I walked away, and pretended for all this time that he would go away if I just ignored him." She dropped her head, ashamed of herself. "That was stupid. Like a child."

Kate soothed her. "He made you afraid again, like when you were a child. That's a perfectly natural response, isn't it?"

Seffie looked up. "It was foolish. I've put Tino in danger."

"What's the threat to Tino?" Will asked.

"Mateo wants him. Or rather, he wants money for him. For giving him up." She used finger quotes on that last, emphasizing the absurdity of Mateo's words.

"So you've spoken with him?"

"I confronted him today."

Both Kate and Will reacted to that, but Seffie waved their concern away.

"He knows everything about Tino." Seffie looked at Kate. "He was here for two weeks before I even saw him. He knows about the farm and Tino's art class schedule." She looked down at her chocolate. "I tried to prevent that. Once I saw Mateo, I stayed away from Tino. But it was already too late."

"How do you know when Mateo got here?"

"A friend." She met Will's eyes. "Trevor saw him, the day of my birthday."

Kate stroked her back. "You were with Sadie and Tino that day. So Mateo already knew where to find Tino. This isn't your fault."

"I've made matters worse, though."

"Here is where we're at, Sef." Will spoke brusquely, in a way that was comforting rather than critical. "I say let's get to Leet's and talk about what we need to do."

Canaan hit a couple buttons and Will answered after a single ring.

"Yeah?"

"Sef's in trouble."

"Yeah. Tino, too. I've got Sef, and we're headed out to Leet's place now."

Canaan hit the brakes before he left the farm road. "You've got Sef?"

"That's what I said."

Canaan wanted to kiss Seffie for going for help, and slug Will for being the one she thought of first. He didn't speak until he got over that second part. "Okay. We'll meet you at Leet's."

"We?"

"I've got the kid."

Will paused, though Canaan could tell he was on the move. There was something said about a car seat in the background. "The kid? You mean Trevor?"

"Yeah."

"*You*'ve got Trevor."

"Yeah." They were on the road now and Canaan glanced over at his passenger. "He's okay."

Will huffed out his amusement. "If you say. I gotta get the sprout because, of course, her mother's gotta be in on this. But, dude—you're armed, right?"

"Yes."

"See you in a few."

"Yeah." Canaan closed the phone.

"That was the deputy?"

Canaan looked over and lifted a brow.

"It was you who had him check me out, right?" The kid didn't miss much. He answered the question in Canaan's glance. "My dad's a Special Agent. He taught me some stuff. What I don't understand is why."

Canaan thought it was Sef's story to tell, but he also figured Trevor had a right to know at least some of it. "Sef told me she was involved with you."

Trevor took a minute, watching out the window. "She'd

been sexually abused. She said she wanted to try it in the sack with someone who felt safe to her."

Jesus. Was he the only moron? Canaan grunted. "I guess."

Trevor eyed him again. "It's kind of hard to imagine she chose you as someone safe."

He grunted again. "Exactly."

"*That*," Trevor said with a lot of emphasis, "is *not* what I meant."

They were silent for a couple miles. Canaan thought about the kid, the way he moved, the way he'd handled the rifle, the way arming up and heading out on a mission didn't seem to faze him. "Martial arts training?"

"Karate. A little aikido."

"And weapons?"

"I can shoot."

"You should have told me back at farm. We could have armed you."

"I'll take your backup piece if I need it."

"By which you mean, I'll hand it over to you should the occasion arise."

Trevor met his gaze steadily, but spoke insultingly. "Sure."

Canaan laughed. "You're okay, kid." He turned up Leet's long drive. "Forensic medicine, I'm guessing."

"Ay-yuh."

When he brought the truck to a stop, he put a hand on Trevor's arm before either of them opened a door. "One thing, though."

Trevor lifted an unimpressed brow. "Yeah?"

"You can't have Sef."

Will took charge as soon as Leet let him in. Sadie was hovering, her distress obvious. He gave her a quick hug and then handed her over to Kate. He took the baby from his wife and put her into Seffie's arms without apparent thought.

"Let's take the table." He pointed to the long dining room table that sat along floor-to-ceiling windows facing the dark of Leet's lovely backyard. "We'll wait a minute before we start. Canaan's on his way," he said.

Seffie's breath caught and she looked up from snuffling Vivienne. "Why is Canaan coming?"

"Because—"

"Because I am." That was Canaan's grim voice from beyond the doorway.

"Because your friend Trevor brought him in." Will finished his sentence as he checked out the two who had come into the room behind Leet.

Seffie met Trevor's gaze first. He looked back steadily, with no apology, until Seffie gave half a nod of acceptance. *Grudging* acceptance.

Then she looked at Canaan. She'd known he was a warrior, had believed it, accepted it, she thought. Now she was seeing it.

He looked dangerous. He clearly *was* dangerous. It was battle dress he wore, and the somberness of his face matched it. His dark eyes were flat as her gaze moved to his. Instinctively, she tucked the baby closer into her shoulder.

"Why are you here?"

He walked close to her, close enough that the difference in their heights meant a lot. Quietly, he spoke to her, as though they were alone. "You should have come to me first, Sef."

She had to work to meet his gaze. It hurt, *hurt* to look into those dark eyes. "I don't see how it involves you."

"I do." Will spoke bluntly into their conversation. He nudged a shoulder into Canaan's. "Back off. Sef, he's who I go to for the kind of help we might need. Cane, whatever you need to deal with, that comes later. Both of you, stand down and sit down." He pointed to the table.

Seffie gave Canaan one more glare and then followed Will's instruction. Canaan didn't—he moved toward the table but sort of hovered over it, not sitting. Near Sef's shoulder, he mostly faced the windows but was turned enough that he could see the door, too. Seffie sighed, realizing his strategy. Aware that he stood guard—over the house, the grounds, and, most of all, her.

Everyone else took a seat. Leet sat next to Sadie across the table. He had one arm around her shoulder and clasped her hand in his lap with his other hand. Kate settled in on Sadie's other side and took her free hand. Trevor walked to the table and, despite Canaan's glower, took the chair to Sef's left.

Will continued his in-charge role. "This is Trevor Jorgensen." He pointed to and named everyone Trevor wouldn't have met. "He's a friend of Sef's."

"And, BTW, he made you, dude."

Will gave Canaan a look that would have been enough to quell Sef, but Canaan just met him glare for glare. When everyone had settled at the table—except for Canaan, who continued to loom over her shoulder—he started what Sef could only consider a briefing.

"Tino's biological father—" Canaan muttered out a more profane description that earned him a suppressive scowl before Will continued his summary. "Is a guy named Mateo Silva. He's here and has been following—"

"*Stalking*," Canaan corrected.

Will put his hands on his hips. "Liberty, you can shut the hell up or I'll show you the door myself."

Canaan crossed his arms over his chest and leaned his weight forward, eyes on Will in challenge. There was a charged moment before Kate stood. "Sef," she said. "You know this part. Hand Vivvie to Canaan and help me get coffee for the table."

Seffie looked from Kate to Canaan, having to wonder if the woman was crazy.

Then Canaan took in a breath and sighed it out. "You're right. Thanks, Kate. Sorry, everybody. Here, sprout." Just that quickly, the warrior was gone and the gentle Canaan Sef knew was back and putting his hands out for the baby. Sef held Vivvie back for a moment until Canaan lifted a brow in impatience. So maybe the warrior was only pushed to the back burner. A little reluctantly, she handed the baby over. With a nod, Canaan settled into the empty chair next to Sef's and tucked Vivienne into his shoulder. Somehow, the picture wasn't wrong, even when Seffie caught sight of the handgun secured at the back of Canaan's waist.

Coffee was already brewing in the kitchen, and a tray was set with nuts and olives and cheese, so Sef and Kate were back in a couple minutes. Sef figured she was probably glad to have missed it as Will filled the others in on her history. He paused as the women passed coffee around and then took their seats. Leet rose and came back to the table with a bottle of Irish whiskey that some added to their coffee.

Seffie noted that neither Will nor Canaan did.

Once everyone was settled again, Will resumed. "I want Sef to tell us from here. She confronted Mateo today."

"Jesus." Canaan said it under his breath, but not that much, and he was looking at her in offended objection when she glanced up. "*Really*, Sef?"

She bit back a strong urge to tell him to bugger off. On her other side, Trevor took her hand. Of course Canaan noticed that and she heard him curse quietly again, but he was hampered by the baby he held. Sef tipped an imaginary hat to Kate.

"Tell us, Sef," Trevor said gently. But she hadn't missed the glance of understanding he'd shared with Canaan. Here was another man who thought he should have been with her when she spoke with Mateo. "This isn't your fault, so don't feel bad."

Though he made no obvious movement, Seffie knew that Canaan bristled with frustration at Trevor's words, at the fact that it was Trevor and not Canaan offering comfort. Sef almost laughed. But, despite Trevor's reassurance, Seffie felt fully responsible for this awful situation. She struggled to suppress tears.

Kate saw her effort. "Trevor's exactly right, Seffie. There's absolutely no blame on you. You had the misfortune of being at the mercy of a villain when you were a child. You didn't have anyone to help you in the past, when adults should have been looking out for you. But you have all of us now. Mateo is an evil man, but no more than that. He doesn't have magical powers. This time, you can defeat him. You could even without us. But we're all here to help you."

Seffie took a moment to let that settle in. Then she found her strength and looked around the table, meeting the gaze of everyone there in turn. Including Canaan. "Thank you. Every one of you."

Some nodded, encouraging her. Trevor propped his arm on the back of her chair, his hand resting on her shoulder. Canaan looked prickly again, but Trevor ignored him and gave her a gentle squeeze.

Kate rolled her eyes, but she put her hands up to take the baby back. "Ignore them, Seffie," she said. "Just tell us what happened with Mateo. Tell me."

Settling herself into Kate's encouraging gaze, Seffie spoke calmly. "He acted all offended that I gave up 'his son' to Sadie and Leet. He threatened to take Tino. He knows Tino's schedule. He knows about Tino's art class and the farm, that there are only women there and 'a cripple.'" She used finger quotes to indicate they were Mateo's words.

Will and Canaan exchanged a look—satisfaction rather than offense—and Sef had to wonder if she would ever understand men.

"I denied that Tino is his. I never named him as the biological father. I never said it to my mother, or to anyone." She looked at Sadie, and knew they were both remembering their first meeting when Seffie was fifteen and pregnant. "Today, I told him that nine months before Tino was born, I got drunk at a frat house and had sex with several boys. That I didn't know which of them was the father."

"Nice try. Bet he didn't buy it," Trevor muttered.

Sef looked at him and shook her head.

"All it would take is a DNA test," Canaan put in.

It was quiet around the table for a moment, until Will spoke. "Which he could only get by admitting to a felony offense."

Sef looked up at him. "He said I only had until five years after I turned eighteen to press charges. That's why he waited until now."

"He showed up on your twenty-third birthday," Trevor pointed out. "This guy's a real douche." He looked at Seffie. "Not that we didn't already know that."

"Is that right, Will?" Leet asked. "Is there nothing we can do legally? Are you saying a freaking rapist—" Leet paused as others took in a breath. "Sorry, Sef. But you understand that's what he was, right? What he is?"

Trevor squeezed her hand and rubbed her shoulder a little until Seffie nodded.

Leet went on more gently. "There's nothing that can be done against him?"

Will lifted a shoulder unhappily. "We may have some other avenues, but the *douche* is probably right about this. It depends on the individual state codes, but it's essentially true in Vermont. It appears Silva isn't an idiot. It's different if the abuse starts at under age thirteen. And Sef, you said he started to hurt you after you turned thirteen, right?"

Sef nodded again.

Canaan cursed. "How much after, Sef?"

She didn't answer.

"Sef." Canaan was impatient, angry. "It was your fucking birthday, wasn't it?"

"*Jesus,*" Trevor breathed.

Canaan stood and paced at the head of the head of the table, like he was unable to stay still. "This guy needs to die."

Will tracked him with his eyes. "Not that I disagree, but I'm gonna act like I didn't hear that. Suck it up, Canaan. We'll find a way to put him away. And"—he raised his voice over Canaan's automatic objection—"we'll figure out how to make that okay for all of us."

"There is one thing that might help," Sadie said. She'd been quiet up till then, obviously anxious and worried. But she sat up straight now and Sef remembered what a strong woman she was. "I spoke to the social workers at the clinic when Seffie first came in. It was a concern because she was so young. *You* were so young, Sef." Sadie paused and waved away the difficulty of speaking both to and about Seffie. "CPS—Child Protective Services—gets involved in situations like this. Very commonly, when a fifteen-year-old girl is pregnant, there's a matter of abuse. It's almost by definition. A case is opened, the home is investigated. By the time Seffie first came to the clinic, she was already living with her aunt. CPS spoke to your Aunt Rosa, honey." Sadie reached across the table to take Sef's free hand. "The report that CPS filed listed Mateo Silva as the likely...perpetrator."

CHAPTER NINE

Sef took a breath like she'd been shot. Canaan was behind her as she stood, and he put his hands on her when she swayed. By the tiniest bit, she leaned into him. Even if he only imagined that, at least he had her out of Trevor's reach.

She spoke to Sadie. "You knew. I didn't think you did."

"We guessed is all, Sef. It wasn't hard to make the right guess."

"You wanted me to tell. I remember. You said the truth was usually best." Sef put her fingers to her lips and leaned a little more. "I wasn't brave enough. Maybe I could have ended this then. What if he's done this to other girls? That would be my fault."

Canaan gripped her arms above the elbows, barely stopping short of shaking her. "It's no one's fault but his, Sef. You did what you had to, to survive. Sometimes saving yourself is all you can do. And when that happens, none of the rest of it is on you."

Sef turned enough to look up at him, and Canaan had the feeling it was the first time she'd seen him—*really seen him*—since he'd walked in the room. He met those pretty blue eyes for as long as he could, then he tucked her in, her back against him, cradling her a bit in his arms. If she couldn't see him, well then, she couldn't *see* him.

"Canaan's right," Sadie said. "This isn't your fault. And anything Mateo Silva has done, before or after he knew you, is also not your fault."

Sef took a deep breath and let it out. Then she took hold of his wrists to open his arms. There was nothing he could do but let her go. She stepped away and took her chair again. But before she spoke, she brought his chair in and waited for him to sit.

"I understand that—mostly," she said. "Thank you all,

again."

She took another big breath and ran her gaze around the table. "Of course, he doesn't care about Tino. What he wants is money. When I told him I have none, he said I should talk to you, Sadie. He said you'd be willing to pay, that you'd have access to Leet's money."

"He's right about that anyway," Leet said, and then kissed Sadie's temple and gave her shoulder a squeeze.

"He said when I saw him again, he'd have a bank number for me."

Canaan leaned his elbows on the table. "You can't pay him."

Leet shrugged. "It might be simplest. And we have money."

Canaan knew that was true. Leet had a really decent, if not spectacular, salary from his football career, and now he was selling his crazy cool tree sculptures for scads of money. Plus, the senior Hayeses were likely rolling in dough if it came to it. That wasn't the point. He shook his head. "Tell them, Will, Trevor. You guys would know. That's a kind of blackmail that would never end."

Will nodded. "He's right, Leet. Even if he never bled you dry, he'd keep coming back. He'd be in your lives forever."

Then Trevor spoke. "Plus, this guy needs to be in jail." He looked across Sef to Canaan. "If we can't kill him."

Damn. He really did like this kid. And he appreciated for Sef's sake that someone besides his all-PTSD-self would point out the obvious. Some folks just deserved to be dead.

Trevor went on, speaking quietly, looking intently at Seffie. "Canaan and I will do it if you want, Sef. We can make it so Will would never know."

"Jesus Christ." Will swore and made eye contact with Canaan. "He's another one of you."

"Yeah," Canaan said. "I like him." He went with his gut and put his arm around the back of Sef's chair, knocking Trevor's hand away. "Trev's right, Sef. You say the word and it's done."

Will's hackles were showing, but he kept his silence, giving Sef the chance to weigh in. Canaan knew that was a big deal for him, and took it as a sign of respect for Sef and what she'd survived. Essentially, he was agreeing that Sef had the right to make the call.

She smiled wryly, acknowledging Trevor and then looking at Canaan. "Thank you both. I appreciate that you're willing to stand up for me in this way. Really, I very much do. You say it as though it would be a simple thing to ask, but I know it wouldn't be. It wouldn't be simple for you, Canaan. And for you..." She looked back at Trevor with a fairly disapproving frown. *Hah!* "For you, it would just be wrong."

She looked around the table, taking a minute at it. That gave Canaan a little time to think about what she'd said. He had to wonder why she'd think it would be wrong for Trevor, but "not simple" for him. He looked up to see Kate watching him with a little excited glimmer in her eyes, like she was having a hot shrink moment. He sighed and figured he'd be talking to her again soon.

He turned his attention back to Sef as she started to speak.

"I'd like to put that option on the back shelf."

Silence around the table gave recognition to the fact that she really hadn't said no to it. Canaan realized that, for the first time, most of the people surrounding her were truly seeing that the strong, competent, content woman they knew had a gravely wounded heart. Only Kate, he noticed, nodded her approval.

"Let's see what we can accomplish through legal means."

Canaan put his hand on her shoulder, as proud of her as he could be.

Sef sat back while they talked, aware more than anything of Canaan's soft touch on her skin. Trevor held her hand again, but that was nothing more than the warm supportive touch of a friend. Though there was some stuff to think about there. Trevor had proved himself way not as uncomplicated as he'd seemed. He'd taken it upon himself to go for Canaan, and she kind of shuddered to ponder what had passed between the two men.

She realized she'd stopped thinking of Trevor as a boy. Hearing him calmly assure her that he could take care of killing a man—for her—in some untraceable way pretty much took the boyhood shine off his cheeks. He wasn't exactly what he'd seemed, no. But he was her friend. Of that there was no doubt. Among all else, his touch said it.

Canaan's touch said something else. She hadn't missed that little tussle behind her back, when Trevor's hand on her chair had been replaced by Canaan's. The weight of it on her shoulder rested lightly. But she could feel his thumb on her skin at the neckline of her blouse, and two fingers at the other edge, on her bare upper arm.

She heard the discussion. They talked about hiring security, about how long that might be needed and how a boy was to live that way. There was mention of lawyers, talking to judges. Leet complained once that they might have been proactive, avoiding this situation, if Sadie had told what she knew about Silva. Sadie stood him down with firm words about HIPAA and her patients' privacy. They argued about parental rights until Will finally said bluntly that most states didn't limit paternal rights even in the case of rape. Leet suggested travel, taking Tino away for the summer.

The conversation circled around her, like a threat knocking at her door. But she felt safe, tucked up warm and tight in...in the shelter of Canaan's touch. That was what really took her attention, nearly all of her consciousness. She didn't think he moved his fingers there on her shoulder, where he touched her skin. There was a pulse, though, like a warm stroke, not movement so much as energy. He was canted toward her, and she felt taken in, protected, surrounded by him. It was such a remarkable comfort that she longed to tumble into it, into him.

She felt like he was there with her, in that place of comfort and shelter, like he'd formed a little force-field around them, separating them from the others. It was such a powerful feeling that it took a moment for her to understand that he'd spoken—not just to her, not quiet words of the love she was feeling, but to the table at large.

Silence had fallen there before she processed what he'd said.

"Kidnapping's still against the law, right?"

Nobody spoke, but all eyes were turned to Canaan. He gave a little squeeze to Sef's shoulder—an apology. He was pretty sure he'd had her there, nearly tucked into his body, certainly surrounded by his energy. He regretted having to pull her out of that little cocoon he'd built around them. Regretted having to leave it himself.

"He's got no legal right to Tino now, right? Sadie and Leet are Tino's lawful parents. For Silva to have a legal right to him would take a lot of doing, yeah? A court process and all. So, if he took Tino now, that would be kidnapping—a crime. Am I right? Will?"

Will looked at him for a long moment, and Canaan was sure he reluctantly got the gist. He spoke slowly, his way. "Yes, you're right. But I'm pretty sure the point for these folks is to keep Tino safe, not use him as bait."

Canaan could see it as others around the table got the idea of what he was proposing. There was a lot of objection forming. He spoke first. "Think about it. We'd set it up. We'd have control. And Tino is a strong little guy. He can handle it. Right, Teen?"

He spoke those last two words loudly, looking up at the reflection in the window.

"Y-yes."

The word was spoken somewhat hesitantly, the voice small, a few seconds before he saw Tino's head—and Jace's—peek through the railing from the balcony above that connected the upstairs bedrooms. He turned around to look directly, as everyone else at the table was doing.

Leet sighed heavily. "Come on down here, boys."

The brothers stood and came down the stairs. Jace had his hand protectively on Tino's shoulder, and they both moved athletically, gracefully—very much like their adoptive father. Leet stood and pulled out the chair beside him for Jace, and Sadie pushed back, obviously expecting Tino to come to her. But he stopped before he circled around the table to her and looked at Canaan.

"I can do it, Canaan."

"I know you can, buddy. We'll just have to talk your moms into it."

"And his dad."

Canaan looked up into Leet's stern eyes. "Yeah." But he

gave a little nod to the kid, who scurried over to climb into his Sadie's lap. Tino didn't object at all to the hug Sadie gave him, though Canaan could tell he was half strangled by it.

Leet stayed on his feet behind Sadie, and it turned out Jace joined him there. They were united as a family, loving and strong, with Leet's hand on Sadie's shoulder and his arm around Jace.

Canaan kept his hand on Sef, and he saw when Leet recognized the situation. Being the truly decent guy he was, he nodded across the table. "You get over here, too, Sef."

Sef smiled, though Canaan knew it cost her. Like it did every day. "Thanks, Leet. I'm good."

Leet shook his head and beckoned. "Nope. I mean it. Come on."

Canaan took charge. "I got her. If she moves over there, then I'd have to move over there, then I'd have my back to the window, and I wouldn't be happy about that."

Leet laughed ironically and lifted both hands briefly in reluctant surrender.

"She knows she's part of your family, and she appreciates the gesture." That raised a few eyebrows around the table and had Canaan reconsidering his words. Or his attitude, at least. "I mean, *right*, Sef?"

"Right."

There was a whole lot of amused tolerance in her voice. Canaan glanced over at her, didn't see any real disgruntlement, and decided he ought to shut up.

This part was for family anyway, and Sadie took over. She kissed Tino's temple and spoke quietly to him. "Tell us what you heard, baby."

"There's a bad man."

"His name's Mateo Silva." Okay, it was for family, but the kid needed to know who he was up against. So Canaan didn't let the various glares he got from the adults bother him too much. Tino was pretty much talking to him, their gazes held across the table.

"He hurt Seffie with sex, and that's how I got born."

Canaan heard the swift sighs of three women. "You getting born was a good thing." Canaan fielded a few more looks, but they weren't so hostile this time.

"That's right. And Seffie was too young to take care of a

baby, so she gave you to us." Sadie spoke with her lips pressed into the boy's hair.

"Like Jace, too."

"Yes, like that."

"Now the bad man wants—"

"He wants money." Canaan spoke bluntly, sure that Tino needed to be certain about this. "He doesn't want you, a boy who could be his son, a boy he could love. He doesn't know anything about love. That makes him mean and selfish. He hurts people, and we want to put him in jail for it."

"Nobody loved him when he was little?"

Sadie whimpered, giving Tino another squeeze and a kiss into his hair.

Canaan loved this damn kid. "You're good to think of that, Tino. And maybe it's true. But Mateo Silva is a grown man now. And a man has to be responsible for his actions. Whatever happened to him when he was little doesn't matter anymore. He was a man when he hurt Sef, and she was only a kid. He has to pay for that."

Tino nodded then looked up past Sadie's head to his brother. "I'm gonna be fish bait," he said proudly.

Small chuckles lightened the mood, but Sadie grasped Tino's cheeks for his attention. "No. You are not."

The men around the table seemed to all exchange glances. Will finally left his gaze on Leet.

"Okay," Leet slowly said. "Let's just talk about it."

Sadie looked at him sharply. "No."

"Just thinking out loud," Leet said. "Let's treat it like that for a minute, and see where we get."

"Leet."

The man leaned over and gently kissed his wife, and left his hand on Tino's head when he straightened back up. The couple had a little bit of silent communication.

Sadie sighed. "Okay," she said. "Talk."

Canaan sat back, obviously trying for innocence, until Will gave him an annoyed look and took the leap. "Well, we could wire him six ways to Sunday." He looked at the kid. "I mean you, Tino." That made the boy light up. "Mateo's not stupid, but we don't have any reason to think he's technologically savvy, do we?"

Seffie stirred, uncertain she wanted to be a part of this. Leet might be able to comfort Sadie and convince her that he had the power to keep Tino safe, but Seffie didn't have the same reassurance. Then she realized she did, sitting right next to her. She took a breath and jumped in. "He was in the Army until he lost vision in one eye, but I don't know what he did while he was in. In the time I knew him, he only ever took occasional odd jobs, unloading trucks and the like."

Trevor waved a hand. "We'll have to be subtle about it anyway. All you have to do is watch a couple cop shows to know something about tracking devices."

Will nodded. "True. Still, Silva's Army and work records are things we can check. We'd have to set the trap up well enough that he wouldn't be suspicious. Once he went for Fish Bait here—" Tino beamed again—"we'd have him."

Trevor spoke again, a part of the group. "If he crossed state lines with him, it would be federal." He looked at Will levelly. "I have some connections with the FBI."

Will looked back a bit sourly. "No sh—surprise." He sighed. "That would put Tino in Mateo's hands for a longer period of time—"

"So, no," Sadie interrupted.

"Just thinking it through," Will said. "We have enough of us that we could always keep someone close. We could stop him anytime if Tino was in trouble. But we could make it happen pretty easily, if we can find out where he's holed up. He's been here a while. He's gotta have a place."

"Canaan and I can do that," Trevor put in.

Canaan obviously figured he could manage without help from that quarter. "You've got classes, *schoolboy*."

"Yeah, and you've got...milking, *goatherd*."

Canaan leaned across Sef to give the kid a hard look, but surprised her by cracking a smile. "*Whatever*."

Will cleared his throat for attention. "So, we could make the grab happen on the opposite side of the river from Mateo's hole. Then we can already be waiting for him at his place—and it would be across state lines. Likely, he's found a spot on the New Hampshire side—he's been watching you mostly, Sef. But either way works. I could claim legitimate jurisdiction if the grab happens in county, or if he brings Fish Bait back here."

Tino smiled up at his brother again. "I have a code name."

Sadie gave a sigh of reluctant, obvious surrender, one that Will noted. "You'd be part of an important operation, son. You'd have to take it seriously."

Tino sobered. "Yes, sir."

Then Will winked. "But every man loves having a code name."

They talked longer, brainstorming, sometimes wildly, about how to set a trap. After a while, Sef noticed that, as Sadie rested her head on Tino's, her eyes were falling closed. Leet noticed, too. He interrupted Trevor on some crazy tangent.

"I suggest we sleep on it," he said. "We know we have Tino safe now, and we'll keep him safe until we figure out the plan."

"Good idea," Will said, looking only mildly distracted by the sight of Vivienne at her mother's breast. "We have some recon to do in any case." He stood up. "Trevor, what's he driving?"

"A beat-up gray Ford Focus."

Will held his gaze a little longer, expectant.

"Sedan. Two thousand eight. New York license, TSW 4934."

Sef heard Canaan snort beside her, and Trevor blushed a little and shrugged.

"So he followed us here," Will said. "He was parked down the street when Sef came to our place. I didn't make any effort to lose him." He looked around the group. "You think we can sell this as a party?"

Canaan nudged her arm, clearly aware that Sef's mood had fallen again. She'd been an idiot, going directly to Will, then leading Mateo to Sadie and Leet yet again. "Still not your fault, Sef. We got this for you now." He stood up and gestured toward the windows. "It depends where he's been watching from. We can check from the upper decks."

Will, Trevor, and Canaan left the room. Apparently, both Will and Canaan had brought night vision scopes.

By the time they came back, Sef had cleared the table.

Leet had made a run upstairs in response to a cry from the baby monitor, and now little Grayson was suckling quietly at his mother's breast. Tino sat in a chair next to Sadie, finding room on her lap for his head, his eyes dropping closed. Leet and Jace sat close together, talking football.

Sef knew Leet thought she wanted to be part of his family, and, to an extent, she did; she *was*. But more, what they had—Leet and Sadie, with their love for each other and their children—was what she wanted for herself. Not their family, but hers. She knew Canaan had caught her watching. She could see the comprehension in his eyes.

"Mateo's out front, in the trees along the drive. Looks like he's been there all this time," Will reported. "Canaan had a better idea than pretending this was a party," Will went on, speaking to the group. "We need to talk about it. Sadie, when you're done there, it would be best if you took Tino off to bed. Jace, too."

Sadie looked up and studied Will's face. The baby was all but asleep at the breast, so she popped him off and tucked herself back together. With Grayson against her shoulder, she ruffled Tino's hair. "Come on, sweet pea. It's time for bed. You too, Jace."

Jace looked like he was going to object, but he got shot down by both his parents without a word spoken. He sighed and then nudged Tino to his feet. Everybody exchanged good-nights as Sadie herded the small group up the stairs. Tino instructed his brother about using his new nickname as they went.

Will motioned everyone else to sit again. "We're going to let Mateo think this was Seffie coming for help—and not getting it."

Leet spoke first as they all thought about it. "What does that gain us?"

"It will make it look like Sef's on her own," Canaan said. Sef had the sense he was watching her carefully. "It will make Mateo bolder, thinking all he has standing against him is a *girl*."

"That's how he thinks of me," Sef said quietly, and Canaan nodded. "You mean I should act like Leet isn't willing to pay him off."

Canaan nodded again.

Sef thought it through. "You think that will press him to actually take Tino then. Why would he do that, when he thinks Leet won't pay?"

Canaan spoke slowly, watching her. "Leet doesn't want to pay because he thinks Mateo is a half-blind, drunken loser. No threat."

"So he'll have to act, to prove himself a man."

Canaan nodded. "You'd have to sell it, both of you. Right here. Tonight. In the driveway."

Sef looked at Leet and took a breath. "I'd be angry. Like you didn't care about Tino because he's not really yours."

Leet's nostrils flared at the insult.

Will spoke for him. "You're brash, Leet. You've had a couple. You don't mind calling Tino yours, and no washed-out, has-been grunt is going to take him from you."

"Yeah," Leet said, looking at Sef. He didn't like it either. And Sef understood why Will had sent Tino and Jace away. Even Sadie.

Canaan was unhappy, too. Sef could hear it when he spoke next. "It's probably best for Trevor to be the one comforting you, Sef. We'll take you home in my truck. Will and Kate can leave in their car later."

Will nodded. "We keep eyes on Tino all the time, with at least two adults within reach of him anytime he goes out of the house. As much as possible, we try to make that look natural—like we aren't making any special effort to protect him. Like we don't really see a threat. We'll get things set and be ready to bait the trap by three days from now. Agreed?"

Everyone nodded or murmured assent. "Let's roll then."

As they stood and moved toward the door, Kate slipped her arm around Sef. "Remember, this is acting. It serves a purpose, that's all."

Sef nodded, appreciating Kate's insight. "I know how to act," she said, wryly.

Kate looked at her—wisely, like she saw things—and nodded.

Canaan had his hand on the door. "I'll go first. I'm impatient, ready to be out of here. Then Sef and Trevor come, Sef reluctant, Trev urging her along. Leet, you step outside the door, but don't speak, or you either, Sef, until Sef and Trev get close to my truck. That will be reason for you to be loud, so Mateo will hear. Got it?"

The others nodded, but Canaan waited for more from her. "Yes," she said. "I'm ready."

His dark eyes on hers, he touched her cheek softly before he opened the door.

As he stepped outside, for the first time, Sef saw him limp.

It was late when Seffie tucked herself into bed. The Hayes house was dark but for the lights on the front porch and in the hallway that were always left on for her. She turned off the hall light herself at the top of the stairs, and did no more than light the bathroom while she made brief work of getting ready for bed.

Then she slipped into bed, her nearly nude body very aware of the plush mattress and the smooth, expensive sheets that were the norm in the Hayes household. So very, very different from the beds of her childhood. Sometimes, there wasn't even a bed, but a haphazardly made up sofa. Never had she had this level of comfort.

But more, she felt *safe*. In a way she hadn't, even in this very bed, since Canaan had left.

She thought about her day and felt she'd lived through an eon. Facing Mateo—with strength, for the first time. Seeking help from Will—she had, in fact, thought of Canaan first, had longed for it to be Canaan she could go to. Then seeing him there, at Leet's, as though it was exactly right that he should be at her side.

Those surreal moments outside Leet's house, hurling horrible words at him as Trevor held her back, dragging her, in the end, to Canaan's truck.

Driving away, they had her tucked between them, Canaan's broad shoulder hard against hers. Trevor might have given her a break—he wasn't so big, didn't need *all* of that space in the shotgun seat. But he took all of it and more, pressing against her from his side, no doubt solely to irritate Canaan.

They all three watched, from three separate rearview

mirrors, as Mateo followed.

His presence behind them made Sef shudder, but pleased Trevor and Canaan.

The only conversation, once they'd both reassured Sef that she'd played her part well and given her a pat to acknowledge what it had cost her, was between the two men, and it was all about tactics. The stalker would be stalked, tonight. Canaan would take Trevor back to his car—left, apparently and, to Seffie, bizarrely, at Canaan's A-frame—and then drive Seffie home. If Mateo followed them as far as the farm, then Trevor would be able to pick up his tail. Once Sef was home, Canaan could join the game. Potentially, even tonight, they would know where Mateo was staying.

Trevor had briefly argued that, in keeping with the roles they'd meant to convey at Leet's, he should be the one to drive Seffie home. She was pretty sure he'd put that out there merely to force a response from Canaan, which came as a single, blunt, "No."

It was awkward, pressed as she was between the two men. They had a significant animosity toward each other—one that centered around her and, moreover, was largely false. Sef was quite sure Trevor had understood and accepted that she'd declined a relationship with him beyond friendship. Still, he goaded Canaan, blatantly touching her, comforting her. That in itself was beyond her to understand.

Despite all that, they worked and colluded together as like-minded best comrades, if not buddies. It was enough to make her want to pull her hair out.

It had been all business until they'd let Trevor out at the farm. Canaan had given her a dark look as she'd moved, after Trevor's soft—and provoking—kiss goodbye, unfastening her belt and refastening herself into the seat where Trevor had been. Canaan could give her all the dark looks he wanted—it was the first time she felt she could breathe since they'd walked out of Leet's house.

He held his tongue, though, waiting a few minutes until he had a report by cell phone from Trevor that Mateo still followed—a thing both Canaan and Seffie already knew, as they continued their watch in the rearviews—and that Trevor followed him. They traveled in silence for several miles after that, crossing the river and heading south.

Finally, when they neared the Hayes place, Canaan deigned to speak. "I like Trevor." He looked over at her, his face lit only by the blue glow from the dash. "But he can't have you, and I told him so."

Seffie huffed. "Nobody is going to 'have' me, because this is the twenty-first century and I'm not chattel. But whether I'm with Trevor or not is up to me, not you, and, frankly, none of your business."

"It *is* my business, and you know it."

She glared at him in frustration and challenge.

He'd pulled up outside the Hayes house. He left the truck running, but put his arm along the back of the seat and turned to face her. "I think you know I lied when I said I didn't love you. I know I hurt you, and I'm sorry for it—more than I can say. I was a coward about it, and I'd like to be a better man than that. I'd like us to get through this deal with Tino, and then I'm going to try to convince you to forgive me."

Sef thought about those words for long minutes before she fell asleep. There had been many opportunities that night to tell Canaan there was nothing but friendship between her and Trevor, opportunities she hadn't taken. She'd indulged in a little selfish pleasure, seeing Canaan's hackles rise at every touch or gentle word Trevor gave her. It was her anger to-ward Canaan that kept her from telling Trevor to stop pro-voking the situation, or letting Canaan know he had no cause for jealousy.

She was a little ashamed of herself for it—she wanted to be a better woman than that. But Canaan was right—he'd hurt her. And even as he'd apologized for it, even as his words had found some soft, unprotected place in her heart, she'd held back the truth of her feelings.

Climbing out of the truck, looking back at him through the open door, she gave him the one truth she couldn't hold back. "It was you I thought of first. You I wanted to go to."

He'd nodded once, solemnly, before she closed the door.

As she slept, she felt it again. That profound sense of safety she really hadn't known since she'd slept in Canaan's arms.

CHAPTER TEN

Three days later, Seffie picked up Tino from his art class. She took him to lunch—burgers, fries, and shakes at a retro diner with outdoor tables. Then they drove to a nature center that had been organized around an old farm site. It contained a small playground area and walking trails that circled a pond and meandered through woods.

There were a few other cars in the lot, but no one in sight of the playground. Likely, birders and the occasional jogger were scattered along the trails.

Seffie had dressed poorly for the outing. She was in a short skirt and high wedge sandals that were impractical for traversing the mowed field that stretched from the parking lot to the playground. She tiptoed along, stopping a couple times to brush wet grass cuttings from her toes. Tino ran on ahead, little patience for the inconvenience of girl clothes.

There was an open shelter with picnic tables nearby and Sef stopped there, working further at her shoes and, in surrender, bending to unhook the straps from around one ankle. She straightened when a vehicle pulled into the lot, sliding to a halt on the gravel surface.

Canaan launched himself out of his pickup and strode toward her. Though "strode" was the wrong word. His gait was fettered—not just a mild limp, but a severe hitch that had him canted to one side and moving awkwardly, slowly.

His face was grim, his eyes blazing. He was still yards away when he started hollering. "You were with Trevor last night. I saw you with him."

Seffie straightened to her full height—on one heel. She answered in his tone—loud and angry. "I told you, it's none of your business."

"And I told you I was making it my business."

"Go away, Canaan. Leave me alone."

"Seffie?"

Tino had taken a few steps back away from the playground, looking at her in concern.

"Get outta here, Tino." Canaan's words were harsh, and Seffie shot him a look.

She spoke more gently to the boy. "It's okay, Tino. You go on and play."

Tino backed away a little, then turned and ran to the play equipment, scampering the wrong way up the slide.

Facing Canaan again, she lifted her sandal and shook it at him, a ridiculous weapon. "I'm done with this, Canaan. Stop stalking me!"

Canaan moved in, and she threw her shoe, hitting him in the chest when the block he tried to make with one arm failed. He got close enough to reach her, making a grab for her arms. She fought him off and pushed against his chest, hard enough to force him into a satisfying, off-balance step back.

They were distracted from their argument when a battered gray Ford in the lot fired up and drove right off the edge of the gravel onto the field. They watched, unmoving, as it sped across the grass and fishtailed to a stop alongside the playground. Leaving the engine running, Mateo leapt out, circled the car, and grabbed Tino off the monkey bars.

Belatedly, Sef and Canaan moved. "Tino!" they both called. But they moved too slowly, Canaan with his ungainly limp and Sef in her one sandal. "Tino!"

Tino called Seffie's name once as Mateo stuffed him into the car ahead of him. Sef saw Tino kick out, but Mateo managed to push himself into the driver's seat behind the boy, close the door, and skid the car around until it made its way back to the lot and then out onto the road. Uselessly, Seffie ran a few steps behind it, hampered by one bare foot and much too late to help. She watched, her hands on her head, until the car was out of sight.

Then she turned and waited as Canaan walked toward her. He didn't limp at all, and already had in his hand the radio that had been tucked into his belt at his back. He held it out so she, too, could hear Trevor's words crackle through. "I've got him. He's headed north. He's going to cross the river at Fairlee."

Canaan and Trevor had found Mateo's hidey-hole on that very first night. He'd rented an old cabin on the lake that still leased for the summer, one of the few that hadn't been replaced with high-end second homes built by wealthy out-astaters for their summer getaways.

Leet was waiting at that bridge, sitting in a nondescript sedan. His father was in a Bronco, stationed at the bridge slightly further south, a less likely choice. Sadie and Kate were in Leet's convertible Jag, heads covered with scarves, all Thelma and Louise. They were a mile south of the nature center, backup to Trevor in case Mateo had turned in the opposite direction than they expected.

Will, his commanding officer and stepfather, Jeff Anderson, and Trevor's father, SA Jorgensen, were already at the cabin, tucked inside and out of sight. It was Will's voice that came over the radio next. "All right then. We've got Fish Bait on our trackers. Nathan and you ladies, move to your secondary positions. Sef and Canaan, you can come in, too. But nobody gets within sight of his route or the cabin until my say-so."

His eyes still on Sef, Canaan murmured, "Roger" into the radio and hooked it to his belt. "He's safe, Sef," he said, apparently reading the anxiety she wasn't trying hard to hide. Then, with a twist of a smile, he rubbed his chest. "We didn't rehearse you throwing your shoe."

She smiled back, knowing he'd deliberately let it hit him, very aware of how close he stood. "I kind of went with the moment."

He stepped nearer, put his hands on her shoulders, and gently pulled her close. "I like this moment better."

When he wrapped his arms around her, she felt the warmth of his breath against her temple. It took a lot to keep from sinking into that very tempting comfort. She held still against him long enough that she heard him sigh.

He leaned back, looking at her with regret and frustration in his eyes. "Come on then. Let's go watch Will rescue Fish Bait."

With that, he lifted her up and, with no difficulty at all apparent, carried her back to fetch her shoe. Watching her intently, he set her on the table, and knelt to fasten her sandal himself. Slowly. With a lot of touching of her foot and ankle that very likely was gratuitous.

Canaan drove fast, though apparently not as fast as Thelma, because when he and Sef got to the little parking area on the near side of the lake, Sadie and Kate were already there. Leet was there, too, with his arm around Sadie. The trail that circled around to Mateo's cabin was rough and slow going, so they'd all hoped to be in time to watch as Mateo fell into their trap. He figured they'd made it, as all three of them were still leaning against Leet's sedan. They held binoculars to their eyes, each of them only looking over once as Canaan and Sef pulled in.

Climbing out of the cab, Canaan handed Sef the field glasses he kept in a cubby and brought out his own scope. Leaning onto the hood of the truck, he focused across the lake as the gray Ford descended the narrow drive to the cabin. "There he is."

He knew he had a better view than the others, so he described what he saw as Mateo pulled the car right up to the door of the cabin. "Mateo's out of the car and tugging Fish Bait along with him." He chuckled. "Tino's fine. He's on his feet and just kicked Mateo in the shin."

Quick as a flash, Mateo had Tino through the door and there was nothing to report for a few long minutes. Then Canaan laughed again as Tino came outside, faced across the lake and, jumping up and down and waving his arms, signaled the all-clear. Canaan could see Will with eyes on Tino from the door of the cabin, letting the boy have his fun.

The whole group watching celebrated, passing around hugs and smiles. Like the good troops they were, no one made a move to drive over until Will's voice over three radios gave them the go-ahead. By that time, Trevor and Leet's father had arrived, and Canaan wasn't even surprised to see Leet's mother drive up in a Mercedes with Sadie's moms on board.

Everyone reorganized into various vehicles—Sadie was riding with Leet now, and the Jag was staying where it was rather than risk its sleek finish on a rough gravel road—and a caravan of happy Tino fans wended its way around the lake.

Somehow, Sef had gotten away from him, and Canaan was disgruntled to find his only passenger in the truck was Trevor. They had the satisfaction of a successful shared mission, so Canaan found it hard to hold a grudge against him. He was nearly certain that Trevor didn't really stand in the way between him and Sef.

Mateo's cabin was at the very end of the rustic road—a good thing, because the line of cars in no way all fit into the small parking area and ended up pulled marginally along the edge, blocking any further passage. When Canaan joined the group in the yard, Tino caught sight of him and launched himself forward. Canaan caught him in the air, gave him a big hug, and settled the kid on his hip. With his arms hooked around Canaan's neck, Tino fired away with details of his adventure.

The others gathered around to listen, and Canaan was aware of many eyes on him. He knew that Tino had been passed around for hard hugs—both his mothers first, then Leet, then all of the grandparents. It was sweet and a little awkward, with all of the kid's family there, that he was the one Tino most wanted to rattle on to.

He understood it, though, the high of a successful operation and the urge to recount the details of it with comrades. So he stepped into the circle as Tino chattered, hoping to look like part of the family.

Tino had played his part well, putting up enough resistance to make it look real, while making no honest attempt to escape. He'd held back his best moves, he assured Canaan, though he did connect with the enemy's shin once and managed a box to the ear.

The whole crowd was entertained by Tino's proud retelling. They quieted, though, as there was movement at the cabin door. The senior Jorgensen appeared first—Canaan had met him the day before, when Jeff and Will and he had come over the back of Hayes mountain by four-wheeler, sneaking up to Leet's house in order to wire up Tino with tracking devices. Jorgensen had even shot an implantable device under the skin of Tino's arm, a guard against the possibility that Mateo would take the precaution of discarding the watch they fastened at his wrist or tossing his sneakers, where they'd secured another device.

Jorgensen walked ahead, and Mateo came next with his hands cuffed behind his back. Federal agents had retrieved the vehicles that had been parked out of sight and waited now at the road to take the prisoner away.

Canaan took a couple steps and handed Tino over to Leet, then moved closer to the path Mateo would walk. Trevor moved, too, seeming as though to greet his father. It turned out that Mateo had to squeeze through between Canaan and Trevor.

Unexpectedly, the prisoner took a sudden fall, landing hard on his face, unable to protect himself with his hands. Canaan and Trevor both leaned over him, giving him a hand up. Trevor was making noises about how he ought to be careful, walking while cuffed on such an uneven surface.

Mateo seemed dazed and disoriented when they got him to his feet and sent him moving forward again. Bent and groaning like he was in pain, he moved in a halting shuffle.

Canaan and Trevor met each other's eyes in blunt male satisfaction before Canaan turned back to the crowd that was once again focused on Tino.

He was pretty sure it would be a long while before Mateo walked straight again.

Law enforcement officers and the various witnesses filled the local sheriff's office to capacity. They spent several hours there. Those who had played only minor parts in the day's operation, or those who had only shown up for the very end, were sent directly home. Marta and Joss took Kate along with them, forming a plan to swing by the village to pick up Vivvie from the sitter then start preparations for a picnic at the farm.

They were calling it the Fish Bait and Release party.

The officials needed to talk to Tino and Sadie, and Leet wasn't leaving those two without his protection.

They also wanted to interview Seffie, and, apparently, Canaan wasn't leaving her to face that on her own.

He'd answered a few questions himself. Special Agent Jorgensen had particularly been interested in Mateo's injuries when he fell. He hadn't seen the prisoner trip, he said. And

Silva's condition when he was helped back to his feet seemed
more serious than the fall itself explained.

Canaan assured him he hadn't seen anything out of the
ordinary. He knew Trevor had some fast moves, he said;
there might have been something Canaan missed. Jorgensen
grunted and allowed that Trevor had said almost exactly the
same thing—about Canaan. Which elicited nothing but a
bland shrug.

Sef was certain both her champions had made Mateo pay
just a little for what he'd done to her in the past.

She'd been interviewed by Jorgensen and Jeff Anderson
together. When Canaan had been dismissed, he'd come to
stand behind her and really hadn't moved since then. She
assumed his presence there didn't really alter the course of
her questioning, but it made her feel safer. Both Jeff and
Jorgensen had raised their brows when Canaan wandered
over. Apparently, Canaan's arms set firmly across his chest
trumped their raised brows. With barely audible sighs, they
relented.

At one point, as they approached the topic of Sef's years
of abuse at Mateo's hands, Jeff offered to have her come
back to finish the interview another time. She felt Canaan's
hand on her shoulder then and nodded for the men to con-
tinue. It wouldn't be easier any different day.

They were the last to leave. Even Will had gone when she
and Canaan walked downstairs from Jeff's office. Canaan
treated her carefully, his arm gently around her, as he guid-
ed her to his pickup and helped her in. He reached across to
fasten her belt himself, then stood looking at her. From the
seat of his truck, she was nearly eye-to-eye with him.

"It's been a rough day for you," he said quietly. "But I
think you ought to show up at this party. Everybody there is
waiting to see you, and you need to eat. How about I take
you there for a little bit, then I promise to take you anywhere
you want to go?"

More than anything, she'd have liked him to walk around
the truck and take his seat, so she could lie down with her
head in his lap and close her eyes for a very long time. But
he was right. Very many of the folks at the party were no
doubt anxiously waiting to see that she was okay. She
looked into those dark, trustworthy eyes. "Anywhere?"

He nodded gravely, and she nodded back. "All right then."

The reception when he drove them up to the farm was exactly as he'd predicted. People were sitting around tables, the meal already well underway. But all conversations halted and everyone paused when she approached. The simplest was Tino. He wore someone's old fishing hat—his grandfather's, she guessed—as though it was a crown. He waved a gummy worm at her. "Look," he said proudly. "Grams made dirt pudding. And I had a fish sandwich."

Sef lifted him and gave him a good squeeze, thankful the events of the day were no more a trauma than could be fixed by a special meal. But Sadie was behind him, her blue eyes solemn and concerned.

"I'm okay," Sef said as she stepped into Sadie's arms. They held for a long moment, Sef aware that they were both recalling their long history, the significance they had played in each other's lives.

"Hey, girl." Leet had her next, lifting her up off her feet with a rough hug. After that, Kate gave her a careful, assessing looking over and a long, warm hug. Then it was the moms and the Hayeses and even Will, who gave her a nod and a hug for her part in the day's work.

Finally, Trevor walked up to her, little Rachel Hayes hanging around his neck like she was in love. Leet disengaged his daughter, much to the two-year-old's indignant objection.

Trevor's blush made Seffie smile. She held the smile as their eyes met and Trevor stepped close. He gently and loosely put his arms around her. "I'm gonna go," he said. "I have to meet up with my folks. My mom drove up this afternoon, so we're all going to spend the weekend together."

"Aw, that's nice."

"I'd ask you to come down to the inn to meet my mom, but I think you're going to be busy."

That made it harder to hold her smile. "Maybe," was all she could say. Then she put both hands on Trevor's face. "Thank you so, so much for today. For doing all you did. Your father, too. Tell him I said so."

"Got it. You did good. I'm proud of you."

He leaned in and kissed her, on the lips, softly, but for a

good long moment. When he lifted his head, he stayed close and spoke quietly. "Canaan's watching, right?"

She didn't have to look to know, so she simply met Trevor's gaze evenly. He held it for a good bit before he broke.

"Sorry," he said on a laugh. "I'll start giving him a break pretty soon. It's just, he deserved this."

Sef kind of had to agree. Anyway, she reached up to kiss his cheek and then stepped back.

Trevor said goodbye to the others, getting a sign-of-respect handshake, shoulder thump deal from Will and a perhaps reluctant but similar acknowledgement from Canaan.

Then the moms moved in, settling everyone back at the tables. Marta put a plate in front of Sef while Joss lit torches against the fading twilight. Sef ate with better appetite than she'd expected, sitting between Sadie and Kate, with Canaan, eyes on her, next to Tino across the table. In a little while, Leet and Jace started to make noise about pie.

Before Marta gave them any encouragement, Canaan stood. He walked around the table and put his hand on Sef's shoulder. "Come on."

She got to her feet and, with Canaan close at her side, said a round of goodnights. It appeared everyone thought it perfectly natural that she would leave with Canaan, that he would take charge of her.

With a touch at the small of her back, Canaan walked her around to the passenger door of his truck. He opened it and nudged her forward, taking a second to realize he didn't have her cooperation. He looked at her with a question in his eyes.

"You said you'd take me anywhere I wanted to go."

"Yes," he said. "I will."

She leaned her head in the direction of his A-frame. "I want to go there."

Canaan's nostrils flared on a rough breath. His eyes glittered in the near dark. "You sure?"

Sef nodded. "Mm-hmm."

He took a couple more breaths then stepped back and motioned her on. She heard the truck door quietly close and then his soft footsteps behind her. When she got to his door, he was close enough to reach around to open it for her.

She took a couple steps inside. Perhaps in deference to the crowd outside the farmhouse across the yard, he left the room dark. Without speaking, he walked around her and went into his bedroom. A moment later, he was back and handed her a T-shirt. "Put this on. You can use the bathroom in there." He nodded back to his room. "You've had a day. I want you to sleep tonight, Josefina."

Compliantly, Seffie took the shirt and went to the bathroom. When she came out, Canaan was standing beside his open bed. He wore loose flannels, one leg cut short. He'd already removed his prosthesis and leaned lightly with one hand on his *bō* stick. Watching her, he waited while she lay down in his bed.

He laid the stick on the floor beside the bed, then climbed in beside her. He pulled the covers up, snugging them around her shoulder. Then, with his head on the pillow beside her, he wrapped an arm around her waist and tucked her close against him.

He kissed her hair. "Sleep," he said.

"Will you be here when I wake up?"

It took him a moment to answer. "I'll get up early to do the morning milking. But I'll come back. Okay?"

She grasped his hand where it circled her and kept hold. "Okay."

For all his years on the farm, Canaan hadn't had to set an alarm to be up for the morning milking. He figured he'd learned well enough to sleep with awareness. So it took him by surprise that he woke to full daylight.

It took him a couple more seconds to get that he was waking up, period.

Sef was still in his arms. He was on his back now, and she was curled into him, her head tucked into his shoulder, her arm around his waist, her legs tangled with his.

He'd settled in against her as dark had fallen, freaking thankful that she was there with him, fully expecting—fully, endlessly grateful—to spend the night guarding her as she slept.

He'd fallen asleep. As he thought about it now, he must have fallen into it within minutes. He remembered hearing her breathing change, incredibly heartened that she'd trusted him enough to so readily let go.

Then he was gone, too. With her right there in bed with him.

Jesus.

His arm was tucked around her, and clearly, his body had been aware of hers pressed up against him. It wasn't merely his usual morning...*wood* that was tenting out his flannels. And when she woke, with her leg tucked up there like that, there was no way she was going to miss it.

Then he realized she was already awake. Her hand didn't just rest on his chest but lightly stroked. He squeezed her shoulder gently and spoke quietly. "I have to go. I'm late for milking."

Sef lifted her head and looked at him with those blue eyes. "Joss took care of it. I saw the lights in the barn come on a couple hours ago, so I texted her."

"You told her I was asleep?"

"Yes. She was surprised." Those damn eyes searched his. "You are, too. Why is that?"

Canaan lifted a hand and fingered back her hair, those lush dark curls that fell down onto his chest. He wished he didn't have to answer, but, if they were going to do this thing... "I've never slept with you before."

It took her a minute to process. "You mean you never actually fell asleep?" She saw the answer in his eyes. "Why not?"

He drew a couple quiet breaths, but they were deep enough to have his dick brushing a little more firmly along her thigh. He kind of figured that was noticeable, but chose to act like it wasn't. "I still have nightmares sometimes, Sef. I've been afraid of hurting you." He realized she might think that ship had already sailed. "Waking up in a panic, I mean. Violent."

"Ah," she said. She made a fist of her hand on his chest and rested her chin on it. If she noticed the way that movement had him quivering, she acted like she didn't. "But last night you slept. What do you think that means?"

He had a flash of Kate doing her shrink thing and felt a little uneasy. "You're the doctor. What do you think?"

She grinned and pushed up, sitting cross-legged right beside him. As she settled, he couldn't help noticing that she'd kept her ridiculous little panties on. It was only a glimpse, but, well, he noticed was all. It didn't have to mean anything, one way or the other.

She leaned toward him, elbows on knees, like she was having fun. *Jesus, save him*.

"Maybe you were simply very tired."

Yeah, sure. He'd been so tired some days in Kandahar he could fall asleep standing up. Even then, he wouldn't have slept through this—through milking time, through Sef texting on her phone, *through the fear of hurting her*.

Watching carefully, she waited for his answer. When it didn't come, she continued on—conjecturing. "No? Maybe..." She lifted a shoulder, seeming to have run out of plausible ideas.

With a heavy sigh, he heaved himself up and sat facing her. "I think it means this. I love you." That seemed to capture her attention, but he shrugged it off. "That was easy. It happened at a wedding two years ago. What's changed is this. I feel whole enough, healthy enough, to love you. I think I can trust myself enough not to hurt you. I trust that if I do hurt you in some way—and I probably will, since I don't really have a lot of confidence in my skills with regard to this kind of relationship—if I do, I think maybe you'll be able to forgive me. I might be...*worthy* of your forgiveness."

Sef nodded, seeming to consider. "All right. That sounds good."

She said it like the conversation was done.

"That's it? That's all you need to hear?"

She leaned into him, close. "You've spent the last three days learning what my experience in loving relationships is." She used finger quotes on that "L" word. "Do you really think *I'm* the bargain in this deal?"

"Fuck *yeah*."

That had her grinning. "Well, thanks for that." She took one hand and twined fingers with him. "Do you think I don't wake up screaming sometimes?" She looked at their hands, not meeting his gaze. "It could happen that you'll wake up some night with me clawing at you."

He touched her chin, lifting her head until she looked at him. "It hasn't happened yet. I don't think it will."

"I don't think you'll hurt me."

He knew she didn't understand that the two situations were not the least comparable. "I've killed people, Sef."

Keeping her gaze softly on his, she nodded. "I assume, if you hadn't, you wouldn't be here." She took his hand to her lips and said those words again. "You won't hurt me, Canaan Liberty. I'm totally confident about it."

Flat out humbled that she was willing to take the chance, Canaan leaned in to touch her lips with his. "What about the rest of it?"

"The rest?"

"When I left? When I told you I didn't love you. Don't we have to talk about that?"

"Do you have something to say besides that you were an idiot, you're very, very sorry, and you'll never do anything like that again?"

He saw the twinkle in her eyes and wanted to kiss her brainless. "No," he said. "Nothing."

"Okay then."

Canaan knew himself to be a freaking lucky man. He tangled his fingers in that gorgeous hair again. "Do you want breakfast?"

"Yes," she said, tilting her face into his hand. "Later."

"Later?"

Her eyes darkened. "After."

"After?"

Her brows arched and Canaan decided he just wasn't going to be that dense. So he leaned forward, his hand still clasped at her neck, and took her down.

Seffie drew a couple slow, deep breaths, taking in his scent, accepting the weight of his body on hers. His dark gaze held hers, and she was pretty sure he was doing the same—taking her essence into him, in every way that he could. Like it was a thing he'd been longing for, the same as she had.

He stroked his thumb along her cheek. He was close—his lips a hair's breadth off hers when he spoke. "You love me."

There was the tiniest bit of question in the words. More wonder. A lot more.

"Yes," she said, taking her own hold on him, twining her fingers into a strand of black hair. "Yes, Canaan. I love you."

He brushed his body over hers so she felt him—the hard planes of his chest against her breasts, the fullness of his erection at the juncture of her thighs. His eyes glittered in intensity, almost moist. "That seems like kind of a miracle to me."

And so it was, she thought. That the two of them, both so wounded, would find this bit of heaven, of salvation, in each other. "You love me."

He nodded slowly, watching her carefully.

"That seems like a miracle to me."

"Sef." His voice shook on that one word.

Still held barely above her, still locking gazes, he used one hand to reach under the T-shirt she wore and tug her panties down. She lifted to help, hooking them with her toes at the end to have them gone. Then he worked at the tie of his flannels to release himself. When he was done, he placed himself at her entrance.

They held each other, arms wrapping, fingers clutching, breaths intermingling, as he took her. He went slowly, making his way to her depths, letting her feel every inch of his taking. They both let out groans of pleasure and relief, until he had her.

Penetrated, entirely. Made one with him.

He held there, his breath harsh and needy. His body was coiled, rigid with tension. "Sef."

"Canaan."

He nuzzled roughly at her neck, into her hair before he lifted up to look at her again. "I'm going to ask you to marry me. Not today." He shuddered and stroked, out of her and back in, one hard time. "Not yet. I need to be sure you're sure." Like he couldn't help himself, he did it again, with a helpless growl.

Sef held him hard, both hands gripping into his hair. She arched, bringing him deeper. "I know what my answer is. And it's not going to change."

"Oh, God, Sef." He lost it then and took her with him. He clutched around her, his breathing ragged, his fingers grasping. His hand moved over her—her hip, drawing her leg up around him; her breast, torturing her nipple. His body thrust, filling her again and again, driving her.

In only moments—or forever—she was lost to it. In it. Higher and higher, until each breath was a moan, each moan turned into a wail. At the end, she was crying his name, and he hers. They were grasping and clutching and shuddering as they shattered, as he emptied into her and she accepted him.

He never fed her breakfast. By the time they left his bed, it was more like—lunchtime. They slept again first, after that intense, needy love-making. He fell onto her for long moments, both of them laboring for breath. Eventually, he rolled them, taking his weight off of her, taking hers onto him. But he kept his place inside her, kept that fundamental connection, even as they dozed.

When she woke, his presence in her body was making itself known again. This time, he made slow, easy love to her, adoring her with his mouth, his hands, his body. He brought her to a long, gentle peak once before he joined her in another shared, sweet orgasm.

They showered together after that, and Sef learned how agile Canaan was using his *bō* stick as a sort of staff/cane/crutch when he moved about without his prosthesis. They ate lunch at the farmhouse, with blushes that faded easily in the welcome they received there. Marta hugged them both warmly, and Joss gave Canaan a nod that Sef was sure meant something important to Canaan.

Afterwards, Canaan drove her back to the farm park, where she'd left her car after Mateo had taken Tino. They walked along the nature trails there and then sat at a gazebo, watching fish in the pond leap to catch their own lunch from the air and listening to the frog and bird song around them.

What a lot had changed in the twenty-four hours since she'd thrown her shoe at him.

After a long, comfortable silence, she asked him what he'd done to Mateo during that obviously engineered fall. He lifted a brow in supposed innocence, and she rolled her eyes to let him know she wasn't buying it.

"Did you strike some important chi point or something?"

He chuckled. "No, there's nothing like that."

"You couldn't take a person down that way, using chi?"

He held the smile as he looked out over the pond. "Well, maybe a true master could, but he wouldn't, would he? Because he'd be good."

"Was it Trevor then? I know something more happened than Mateo simply falling."

Canaan sat back and looked at her. He took her hand and kissed it. "Men have vulnerable points. Trevor and I might have had the same idea. That's all I'm saying about it."

"Oh." Sef thought about it. "Ouch."

He had his arms crossed over his chest now and huffed out a breath. "Yeah." Keeping his arms where they were, he turned a little to look at her. "So, will you move in with me? At the farm? I don't see myself creeping up the back steps at the Hayes place to be with you."

She smiled, unable to resist. "I might enjoy seeing that."

He waited her out. *Almost.* "Come on, blue eyes."

"Yes," she said. "I'll move in with you."

CHAPTER ELEVEN

God, he hated goats. Canaan stood at the bottom of the porch and used the mudchucker to scrape the slop off his boots that he'd picked up just crossing the yard from the barn. It was nearing the end of October and there'd been a week of cold rain that had him thinking about looking for work in New Mexico. Maybe even old Mexico.

He climbed the steps and took shelter under the over-hang he'd built onto the front door—a thought he'd had in the summer, when he'd had a beautiful woman standing in the rain on his porch, and had had the sense to implement in September, before the weather went to shit.

He sloughed off his slicker and hung it on a hook, know-ing it would be still damp but not drenched for morning milk-ing. *Stupid goats*. He put a hand out, leaning against a truss for balance while he used the bootjack.

That was all it took to change his outlook. He might hate goats, but he loved his life.

Through the window, he got a look at Sef. She was at the dining table, peering at her laptop, prepping for a big exam she had in the morning. She had her hair tied back and was dressed in jeans and a sweater and bright knit socks, and still looked as hot as could be. She was lit by the fire he'd started for her before he went out to the barn, knowing she'd come home to an empty house. It cast her in a magical little glow.

He was freaking blessed. And he freaking knew it.

The two of them had taken to living together like it was meant to be. She'd made a home out of the A-frame with nothing more than her presence. She had the place filled with textbooks and journals and was as likely to invite her study group to meet there as to join them anywhere else. They cooked some, usually together, but still took a handful of meals a week with Joss and Marta. Without his asking, she respected the sparseness of his room. She'd leave traces of herself—items of clothing, her books, her empty mugs—everywhere but there.

Seffie included him with her friends and joined him when he hung out with his. She didn't fuss when he took time to himself—his workouts, his Saturday basketball, or quiet time in the barn that he spent writing. Obviously, she was busy herself, but he knew also that she was secure in her own life, and confident in his love for her. She wouldn't be needy or resentful just because he had stuff to do.

And vice versa, thank God. Seemingly totally natural about it, not like she was going out of her way to do it, she made him certain of her love. It wrapped around him, kept him warm like the best cold-weather gear ever.

They slept in each other's arms every night, taking only a week or so to get past that fear they both had about their pasts coming to haunt them. They talked about everything, from their daily lives to their traumatic pasts. He'd told her a little bit about his family.

There was only one thing they hadn't talked about, and he was going to change that tonight.

She looked up with a smile, like she always did, when he opened the door. And, like always, she came to him, greeting him with a warm—warming—hug and kiss.

"Mmm. That's good." It was. Good enough to make him forget all about stinky wet goats and shit for weather.

"You're cold," she said, rubbing his hands. "Come in."

She offered to heat up the soup they'd made the day before, while he showered to warm up and get rid of goat stink. She had the table set and candles lit—books and laptop all pushed to one end—when he came out. He'd left his prosthesis off—she really didn't seem to care if he hopped around with his stick.

They ate enchilada soup and talked about their days. Goat drama didn't really feel to him like it compared to learning to save folks' lives, but she acted like what he had to say was interesting, too, God bless her.

She usually studied again after dinner, so she cleared the table and left the dishes in the sink for him to wash later. He waited for her at the table. She knew something was on his mind when she came back and saw him watching her.

"What's up?"

"I have to take a short trip next month. I wondered if you could get a week or so off and come along. You'd need a really nice dress."

She lit up like a kid going to Disney. He'd turned his chair away from the table while she was gone, and she climbed right into his lap. She hooked her arms around his neck and kissed him. "Are you taking me to the CMA's?"

He remembered she wasn't an idiot. "What do you know about that?"

"I know you'd better win song of the year."

He had to laugh at her attitude. "Exactly when did you figure this out?"

She kissed him again. "After that first night I waited for you on the porch. You'd been at the CMT's, hadn't you? You were gone for a few days, and I got a little afraid you had a woman tucked away somewhere, so I checked." She leaned back and took a closer look at him. "Why? Do you think your little goat herding self isn't enough for me?"

"Something like that."

"Because...you're...an..."

She left a space between each word, prompting him to complete her sentence. Finally, he complied. "Idiot?"

"Uh-huh. What's the date? I have to shop."

"First Thursday. I thought maybe we'd stop in Kansas after, see my family."

"Oh." She drew back then, not looking quite so happy. "Do you think they'll like me? Maybe they'll think I'm not good enough for you."

He huffed out a laugh. "Are you shitting me? Likely a good half of them will warn you off me, thinking they're doing you a favor."

She looked at him, more serious in response than he'd meant. "It won't work."

Shit. The damn woman could twist his heart. "I know it." She liked hearing that, he could tell, had waited for him to say it. "Thank you, baby."

Canaan did win song of the year, the award for writers. Faith was very happy with him still, but the woman was less expressive about it this time, when he had Josefina on his arm. Sef was sporting a big rock on her left ring finger and made sure Faith saw it. Canaan didn't bother to point out that Faith had her own man who was a much bigger deal than a goat herder. If Sef didn't already know that, she wasn't going to hear it from him.

Giving her the ring was the best moment of the day, even bigger than winning best song. In their hotel suite, she'd dressed with more elegance than flash. He fondly recalled that hot little red number she'd worn the night he'd first seen her—he'd recalled it many, many nights when he was alone and lonely, and it would always hold a place in his heart.

This was something else. She wore a blue gown that matched her eyes, making them stand out like lasers. The top was strapless, sleeveless, and clung to her curves until it flared out at her waist. Below that, the skirt followed her curves again, down nearly to her ankles. It would have been very demure except for that slit up the right side to her damn hip.

It had nearly bowled him over when she'd walked out of the bedroom, her hair piled on top of her head, striding along in high, silver heels. He'd barely bitten back his first response, which was, *no effin' way she was leaving their rooms in that get-up*. As it was, he'd spent the first half of the night worried that her breasts were going to fall out of that spectacular top, or that the slit up her skirt was going to let go and reveal all.

Whatever woman-magic she had, things stayed covered—enough—as they needed to, and eventually, he mostly relaxed about it. He could only count his lucky stars that he'd managed to cover his first reaction. He figured it would take a man a while to recover from that sort of blunder.

It had been easy, after all. She was freak-all beautiful, and he was stunned once again to know that she was his.

Mrs. Dr. Hayes had shopped with Sef for the dress, and she'd helped him out. So when Sef had walked up to him and he'd gotten his tongue back, he was happy to be able to hand her a box that he was certain held the right things. She oohed and aahed plenty over the diamond and sapphire necklace and earrings. And he had to admit it was a damn moment, fastening that glittery thing around her neck. It stirred a bit of primal pride in him, the way her wearing his bling marked her as his.

But even that wasn't the best. When she'd gotten done smearing her lipstick on his face and then dabbing carefully at tears—apparently, she'd spent some time on her makeup—he took her hands and stepped back, looking her over. "One more thing," he said.

Then next box, he took from his pocket. Like the biggest goner in the world, he'd tucked it into his tux jacket, right over his heart. He held it out to her. She had to know it was a ring box, and her hand shook when she took it.

"Canaan," she said, looking at him rather than the box.

"Yeah," he said. Not the most suave response ever, particularly from a man who—the *fucking world* knew—could write love songs. But it said it all. *Yes. This was right. This was.*

She opened it and, honest to God, damn near swooned. She let out a little moan and actually swayed, enough that he took a step forward and grasped her arms to steady her.

He hadn't stinted. The necklace and earrings were nice, but the ring was just short of over the top. He had money; was pretty sure that, after tonight, he'd have more. He didn't have anything better to spend it on than this. Even so, he'd held himself back a bit. He'd considered his woman and her relatively simple, practical nature. So he'd gone platinum with the band and three carats with the stone, but he'd stuck to a simple design with a Tiffany setting.

Still, it had turned out pretty good, and she seemed to like it. There were enough tears now that he was sure he was going to have to worry about being late as she took the time to repair her makeup.

But it was all worth it, because she loved the ring and she loved him. She told him so—both deals—a few dozen times.

After that, there was a fair chance the reason they were going to be late was that they were about to be naked on the bed for a good long time. At the last minute, though, she cottoned on to the glimmer in his eye and shot him down.

They had places to go, she said. People to be seen by.

Before he gave in, he extracted a promise that the night would end with her in his bed, wearing nothing but the ring.

He was about to cash in on that promise now, and he was pretty sure there was going to be a new best moment of the night.

Oh, they'd partied some. They'd hit a couple private shindigs—Faith and Tim couldn't be said no to—and, Canaan's favorite, a couple of the bars where music was being played by the guys who might be winning their own awards in another few years. But through it all, Sef and he had kept their eyes on each other, totally mindful of the promises that had been made that night.

He got her back to the hotel as quickly as he reasonably could. And when he came out of the bathroom, she was there just as he'd wanted. Naked on his bed, that little sparkle on her finger the only thing she wore.

"Yeah, Mom?"

Canaan and Sef were in the pickup, well past Cheyenne County line. He'd pulled off the side of the road a few minutes back, before his mother's call had interrupted what he had going on in the front seat of that truck.

He and Sef had spent another day in Nashville. He met with his agent, then they had lunch with Faith's band. They'd toured the Grand Ole Opry and, that evening, they'd gone back to the bars for more music. After his third beer, he'd been talked into picking up a guitar, and he'd sung a couple songs to his girl. She'd seemed to think that was pretty cool.

He'd started doing some writing in the house, once he learned that Sef already knew about that part of his life, so she'd heard him pluck a little. She was a decent audience— right up there with the goats. But he hadn't truly sung to her until Friday night.

She expressed her enthusiasm about it in the best of ways, when he got her back to the hotel.

They'd driven Saturday, as far as Kansas City, and would be at the ranch now in another little bit.

But he'd been sitting beside her all day, watching sunlight

glint off that ring on her finger, and, finally, he'd had enough. He'd pulled off the road, practically into one of the fields of the old Gorthy ranch, and shut the truck down. He took Sef's left hand by that ring and pulled it up around his neck. Then he wrapped his arms around her back and kissed the hell out of her.

He didn't know how far he was going to take it. They hadn't seen another vehicle—short of farm implements—in many miles. And a man could work with the space he had in the bench seat of a truck. Sef didn't seem to be planning to call a halt to it—he had a breast in one hand and her jeans unhooked when the damn phone rang.

He groaned out a couple breaths before he answered.

His ma paused, suspiciously like she knew exactly what he'd been doing, *dammit*.

"Hi, sweetheart."

Wow. Way to throw a bucket of cold water on a man. He took another breath. "Hi, Mom."

"Listen. I'm helping out in town. There's a wedding at the church, and they needed a hand with the reception. Will you stop by there first? I'm in the church basement."

"Yeah, sure. Who's getting married?"

He'd had regular calls from all the women—Carlie, Bonnie, and Betsy—since he'd made his last trip to St. Francis, so he was caught up on local gossip way more than he needed to be.

"Oh, it's a new family in town, one of their daughters. You wouldn't know her."

"All right. We'll stop by."

"You still have Josefina with you?"

He huffed out a laugh. "I've still got her. Did you think I might have lost her? Or that she dumped me?"

He could hear the smile in his mom's voice. "Forget I asked. You sounded quite like you were going to hold on to her."

He had his hand on Sef's ass, so little did his mom know.

Again, there was a silence like she knew stuff she shouldn't. "I'm very much looking forward to meeting her."

"Yeah, well, it will only be a few minutes. See ya soon."

"Love you."

He closed his phone and looked at Sef with no doubt obvious regret. "Looks like we're going to have to finish this later."

She was already scooting back to her seat and pulling on her belt. "Much later."

He heard that. "Why do you say that?"

"You're not making love to me in your parents' home."

Somehow, that didn't surprise him. Unfortunately. "Yeah, well, I'm sure we can find a nice warm haystack in the barn. Hay keeps the heat in, you know."

She lifted a brow in her rarely used princess way. "You think you're going to make love to me in a barn?"

He grinned. "*Again*, you mean? I'm sure I can point out the goats that got a look at your bare ass over the summer. They high-fived me in the morning."

The brow rose improbably further. "That's not even a little bit funny."

Sending her a look to let her know the conversation wasn't over, he fired up the truck.

Canaan grumbled about the number of vehicles in the church lot, enough that it was hard to find a place to park. He said he didn't think someone new in town would have such a turnout.

But he'd helped Sef out of the truck and led her through the side door that went to basement before the explanation for it was clear.

Canaan came to a complete stop, his hand gripping hers hard, when they entered the large reception room.

There was no wedding. There *was* a large crowd. Music started to play as they got through the door, and it was country music's most recent song of the year. There were balloons and banners everywhere. One said, *Welcome Home, Canaan*. A second smaller one was angled over it at the end—*and Josefina*. There was another conveying congratulations on his award, and a handful of posters that appeared to be of a younger Canaan with his guitar, singing into a microphone or playing in a band.

Sef was going to get a closer look at those, soon.

But Canaan seemed to be having a little moment of panic, so she squeezed back on his hand and put her other hand on his chest to draw his attention. He looked at her, and she could tell it grounded him a bit. She smiled and nodded over her shoulder. "Go on."

He held her gaze another few seconds, then followed her instructions. He stepped forward into, Sef was sure, Carlie Liberty's arms.

"Hey, Mom." He took the lovely woman with one arm until, with another squeeze, Sef loosened her hand from her grip. He looked back at her once, then gave himself over to it.

Sef watched as Canaan relaxed marginally, smiling as he was hugged next by the women Sef guessed were his sister and aunt. As he moved into the crowd, Carlie came and gave Seffie a hug. With her arm around Sef's shoulder, she gave a play-by-play. Bonnie and Betsy, she pointed out. And then, with a more formal greeting and an exchange of words Sef couldn't hear, Canaan's father.

Bonnie came then, too, standing at Sef's other side. The two women kept up their commentary—Bonnie's husband Henry, the aunts and uncles and cousins. They were suspiciously silent when Canaan turned to greeting friends and neighbors, and he accepted a kiss from a brown-eyed, blond-haired bitch.

Sef didn't have to be told. She could just tell.

Once Canaan had gotten past greeting his dad, Carlie had obviously relaxed. She and Bonnie watched with pride as Canaan moved through the crowd. After a few minutes of it, Betsy came over to introduce herself. Then she took Sef's hand and followed in Canaan's wake, introducing her around.

By the time they got to the brown-eyed bitch, the woman had latched onto the arm of a big hunk of handsome. Sef snidely—and silently—noted that she hadn't been anyone's arm candy when she'd kissed Canaan.

Sef gave her friendliest fake hello, and really couldn't blame Colleen for the fact that her eyes got stuck on Sef's pretty little diamond. Well, not so little. Embarrassingly large, in fact, but how could she complain?

Betsy had been subtle about it, but, eventually, they couldn't avoid meeting up with Canaan's father. Betsy introduced them, and Jake Liberty gave a quiet, correct greeting, accompanied by an equally lukewarm handshake.

Sef decided to begin as she meant to go on. She looked tall Jake Liberty in the eyes. "You must be so grateful every time you see Canaan, Mr. Liberty." She looked at Betsy then. "I was so sorry when I learned that your husband didn't make it home." She turned to Canaan's father again. "We're all so fortunate Canaan is with us, aren't we?"

Jake didn't answer, outside of the reddening of his cheeks. They stood in a little pocket of silence until Seffie heard Canaan quietly say her name.

She'd been aware that he'd looked over his shoulder often, finding her from amongst the crowd of well-wishers. She knew he'd seen when Betsy had taken her under her wing, and that he'd relaxed a little more after that.

But he was watching now, and he had his hand out to her.

Determined that she'd make as much of this happy welcome as she could, she took the few steps to him with a bright smile.

Canaan couldn't hold back a grin as Sef came to him, looking nothing but pleased. He'd seen the exchange between her and his dad, and he was sure it wasn't entirely friendly. But she'd turned to him with pride and pleasure in her eyes, and he was grateful to his core.

It had taken a few minutes among this crowd to accept that the welcome and the congratulations he was given were, for the most part, heartfelt. He'd had his own awkward greeting from his father, and had no doubt that Jake had been under orders from Carlie to be on his best behavior. Then he hadn't reacted in time to duck Colleen's kiss and had to school himself to not look over to Sef like a guilty high school kid.

He felt exactly that goofy, though, as she came to him and put her hand in his. Like nothing more than a smile on her lips and pleasure in her eyes was enough to light up his heart.

Canaan didn't care who the hell was watching. He took her in his arms and went in for a kiss. She stopped him short, though, with a hand against his chest. Then, with a little stern look, she took her fingers and rubbed his lips, like she was rubbing off...someone else's kiss.

Not terribly subtly, when she was done, she brushed her fingers off on his sleeve. She looked up at him then and said, "Okay now."

Stunned to silence, Canaan stared at her. At the same moment he cracked, he heard, of all things, his father's laughter. Like he'd thrown his head back and let loose a laugh he'd been saving up for years.

It was no doubt true, and he'd bet his bottom dollar his mother was watching with tears in her eyes.

Canaan didn't care. With a grin he couldn't control, he lifted Sef up and swung her in circles. He let her down slowly, skidding along his body, until he could reach her lips. Then he kissed her, leaving no doubt for anyone in the room about who owned his heart.

When he set her on her feet, she had a sweet smile on her face and a pretty little blush on her cheeks.

"Now, Sef."

They were totally the center of attention, and that blush got a little stronger. "What?"

"I'm asking you now."

She took a breath, gazing into his eyes. "I told you the answer was never going to change."

"Yeah, but you never really said what the answer was."

"Do you have any doubt?"

He took a deep breath. Was it too much to ask her to make this easy on him? "Just a very little bit," he said.

She looked around, clearly aware of their audience. "Well then, maybe you should ask properly."

That got a couple of hoots and a little crude encouragement. Taking a deep breath, acting like the man he wanted to be, he went to one knee. He took her hand as she smiled, the hand that already wore his ring. "Josefina Claire, will you marry me?"

Sef bent over him, tangling her fingers into his hair. "Yes, Canaan Liberty." She leaned in to kiss him. "What else do you think I would do with you?"

ABOUT THE AUTHOR

Rebecca Skovgaard is a midwife in Rochester, New York. She is a wife (of one) and a mother (of three) and an avid, if amateur, gardener. She loves to write and does so on her laptop whenever she has a quiet few hours or in her head when she walks or gardens or should be falling asleep. She writes romance, where love heals and conquers all, and where you can always trust there to be a happy ending.